Books by Trevor

Abigail Pink's Angel

Peggy Larkin's War

Faylinn Frost and the Snow Fairies

The Wishnotist

Magic Molly (book one) The Mirror Maze

Magic Molly (book two) Gloop

Magic Molly (book three) The Yellow Eye

Magic Molly (book four) The Fire Witch

Magic Molly Christmas Carole

Stanley Stickle Hates Homework

Stanley Stickle Does Not Have A Girlfriend

Magic Molly
The Fire Witch

By

Trevor Forest

Dog Eared Books 2013

Special thanks to Maureen Vincent-Northam for her wonderful editing skills. Thanks also to my favourite artist, Marie Fullerton for the fabulous cover and internal illustrations.
I would also like to thank my Springer Spaniels, Molly and Maisie, for trying their best to be quiet when I was working.
You can find out more about Trevor Forest on his web page;

http://www.trevorforest.com

The Fire Witch

Chapter One

'Molly Miggins, if you aren't down these stairs in five minutes flat I'll feed your breakfast to the birds.'

Molly lay on her back and stared at the ceiling. She wasn't too worried. She knew that sparrows don't like Wheaty Flakes; she tried to feed them some when she was little.

'Birds don't like Wheaty Flakes, Mrs McCraggity,' she shouted. 'Anyway it's Saturday and I always...'

Molly stopped mid-sentence and leapt out of bed. It *was* Saturday and that meant she was going to have her first flying lesson.

Molly showered in record time and raced down the stairs to the kitchen. She pulled back a chair, threw herself onto it, and poured a generous helping of cereal into her bowl.

'Is Granny Whitewand up yet?' she spluttered through a mouthful of Wheaty Flakes.

'I haven't seen her,' said the housekeeper.

'We're going to test out my new broomstick today.'

Mrs McCraggity put a rack of hot toast on the table. 'Don't talk with your mouth full. It's not polite.'

Molly swallowed another huge spoonful.

'It wasn't full; I swallowed most of it before I spoke.'

'Don't be cheeky, young lady. You know what I meant.'

'Are you coming to watch me fly, Mrs McCraggity?'

The housekeeper thought about it for a moment. 'I will if I get time. I've got a lot to do today. Don't you need to get a broom licence first?'

'A broom licence?' Molly's spoon stopped half way to her mouth. 'Why do I need a broom licence?'

'You can't fly without a licence, Molly. Someone will have to take you down to the post office to get one.'

The door opened and Granny Whitewand shuffled into the room.

'Morning, Granny Whitewand,' said Molly.

The old witch yawned a jaw cracking yawn, sucked her teeth back into place and hobbled towards the table. 'Good morning, Millie.'

Molly sighed. Granny Whitewand always got her name wrong.

'It's Molly, Grandma,' she reminded her.

Granny Whitewand sat down at the table and hung her walking stick on the back of Molly's chair.

Molly turned to face her grandmother. 'Mrs McCraggity says junior witches need a licence before they can fly.'

'She's right,' said Granny Whitewand.

'Bother,' said Molly.

Mrs McCraggity placed a china cup and saucer in front of the old witch and poured milk and tea into it. Granny Whitewand splashed in four spoons of sugar and stirred it absentmindedly. 'Something quite important is happening today, but I can't think for the life of me what it is.'

Molly looked up from her bowl with a big smile on her face. 'I'm having my first flying lesson.'

Granny Whitewand drank her tea with a loud slurp.

'Are you, Millie? That's nice.'

Molly rolled her eyes to the ceiling. 'It's MOLLY, Grandma.'

'So you keep saying,' said Granny Whitewand as though she knew better. 'Who are you going flying with? I might pop along to watch.'

'You, Granny,' said Molly. 'You promised to fix up my broom and give me my first flying lesson.'

'Did I?' Granny Whitewand slurped at her tea again. 'Broom? I can't remember anything about a broom.'

'The broom I brought back from my last task?' said Molly patiently. 'It was all in bits, remember?'

Granny Whitewand thought for a while.

'No, I can't remember. But I saw a broom on my bedroom floor this morning. You can have that one if you like.'

'That *is* my broom,' replied Molly, testily. 'You fixed it up yesterday.'

Granny Whitewand made a squelching sound as she sucked on her teeth. 'Did I?'

She finished her tea and rubbed her chin thoughtfully. 'Do you know, I think you're right; I must have been working on a broom yesterday because I woke up in a bed full of twigs this morning. It wasn't very comfortable, I can tell you.'

Mrs McCraggity refilled Granny Whitewand's cup. 'Molly hasn't got a broom licence yet.'

'Of course she has a licence,' said Granny Whitewand. She looked at Molly from under the brim of her hat. 'Haven't you?'

'Er, no. I haven't actually got one yet,' said Molly.

'Well then, you can't fly and that's all there is to it,' said Granny Whitewand. 'You'll get arrested if you don't have a proper licence.'

Molly was getting seriously confused. She was about to reply when her mother came into the kitchen. Molly's mum was a High Witch and taught at the Witch's Academy.

'Good morning, everyone.' Mrs Miggins sat down, poured herself a cup of tea and took a slice of toast from the rack.

'Mum, I'm supposed to be having a flying lesson today but I don't have a licence.'

Mrs Miggins nibbled the corner of her toast. 'I'll give you a lift down to the post office later on, Molly. Granny Whitewand will have to come with us if she's going to be your instructor.'

'Eh, what's that?' Granny Whitewand cupped her hand to her ear.

'I was just telling Molly that you'll have to sign her licence application as you're her instructor, Granny Whitewand.'

‘Am I? It’s the first I’ve heard of it.’

Molly shook her head; Granny Whitewand was hard work at times. She got up from the table and put her bowl in the sink. ‘When are we going, Mum? I can’t wait to get started. I want to be solo flying by next week.’

‘You’ll only get a learner licence to start with, Molly, you’ll have to be accompanied at all times.’

‘That’s not fair,’ said Molly. ‘I can fly it; I flew by myself on my last task.’

‘I’m aware of that, Molly but it’s the law. You can’t go out on your own until you pass your test. There’s more to flying that sitting on a broom you know. You have to be able to fly safely and not be a danger to other flyers. Someone will have to be at your side until you pass your test.’

Mrs Miggins finished her toast and got up to return to her study.

‘Make sure you bring your latest spell book with you, Molly, the one with the *fly* spell in it. You’ll have to prove that you’re capable of casting it because you’re only nine and you’re supposed to be twelve to get a learner’s licence. I’ll be ready to go in about an hour.’

Molly walked back to the kitchen table to make sure that Granny Whitewand had heard, but she was fast asleep in her chair.

Chapter Two

An hour later, Molly, and a now wide-awake Granny Whitewand, climbed into Mrs Miggins' car and they set off for the post office.

Granny Whitewand looked at Molly and smacked her lips. 'I wouldn't mind a nice hot mug of tea while we're in town.'

'You had four cups for breakfast, Granny.' Molly was amazed that anyone could drink so much tea.

'They were little cups,' said the old witch. 'I'm awake now, I need a proper drink.'

Molly frowned. 'We need to get back as soon as I get my licence so we can start my flying lessons.'

Mrs Miggins laughed. 'Granny Whitewand loves her tea, Molly. We'll go to that little café opposite the post office. They do lovely cakes there. You have the rest of the day to practice flying.'

Molly put her elbows on her lap and stuck her chin in her hands. 'If she can stay awake long enough between cups of tea,' she muttered. Granny Whitewand was very old and she needed a lot of what she called, "forty winks". Molly knew she needed a lot more than forty, she counted them once, when Granny Whitewand was asleep in her chair and gave up at nine hundred.

Mrs Miggins parked up behind the post office and helped Granny Whitewand out of the car. Molly ran in front and held the shop door open.

The post office counter was so high that Molly couldn't see over the top of it. Mrs Miggins took a pen from her bag and asked for a learner's broom licence. A woman, with a thin face and pair of tiny spectacles perched on the end of her nose, took a form from a pigeonhole, and slid it under the glass-dividing screen. Mrs Miggins filled in Molly's details and passed it back. The woman examined it and picked up an inky stamper. She tilted her head back and looked around the post office.

'Is the applicant present?'

'I'm here,' said Molly.

The women leaned forward and looked over the counter.

'You're a bit short for flying.'

Molly was indignant. 'I'm just the right height for my age.'

The woman looked at the form again.

'I see you're only nine, this is very unusual, we don't usually issue broom licences to girls under twelve. Are you sure you qualify?'

Molly reached up and slapped her new spell book on the counter.

'I've got the *fly* spell; I'm a grade three witch. The Magic Council keeps giving me tasks.'

The woman examined the spell book as though it might be a forgery. She checked Molly's name and address in the front of the book and then made a big fuss of checking the Academy's official stamp. Eventually she seemed satisfied.

'This is very unusual but everything seems to be in order. Who will be instructing the applicant?'

Mrs Miggins began to explain but Molly butted in.

'Granny Whitewand is going to be my instructor; she fixed up my broom and…'

'Granny Whitewand,' repeated the woman. She filled in a line at the bottom of the form and looked back through the glass.

'Is she present?'

Molly looked around, Granny Whitewand had fallen asleep leaning against the birthday card stand.

Molly tugged at her sleeve. 'Granny Whitewand, we need you to sign the form.'

Granny Whitewand's head snapped back. 'Eh? what?'

'My broom licence, we need you to sign it.'

The old witch shuffled forward towards the counter. The post office official looked at her over her spectacles.

'Is she capable of giving flying lessons? She looks a little past-it to me.'

'Plastic? Who's she calling plastic?' Granny Whitewand leaned on the counter and fixed the woman with a stern eye.

'I might have to get my supervisor to look at this,' said the official. 'Molly might be too young and this lady might be too old.'

The woman turned away and walked briskly through a door at the back of the shop. She returned with a smug look on her face.

'You'll have to come back in half an hour. Mr Stickitt says he will need to make a few phone calls to check your credentials.'

Mrs Miggins put her pen back into her bag. 'Very well but I can assure you that everything is in order. I am the High Witch at the Academy.'

'That's as maybe,' sniffed the assistant. 'But we have to check these things, we can't go handing licences out willy-nilly, or anyone could get hold of one.'

Mrs Miggins led a very disappointed Molly out of the post office. 'Shall we go for that mug of tea while we wait?' she said.

Granny Whitewand smacked her lips. 'Mmm tea. My throat's as dry as a camel's big toe.'

'I don't want tea, or cake. Can I just have a walk around to look at the shops?' asked Molly.

Mrs Miggins nodded. 'All right, Molly, but only for fifteen minutes. Meet us in the café. I'll save you a bit of cake.'

Molly wandered along the street looking into the shop windows. She wasn't really interested in buying anything, she just didn't like the idea of sitting in a stuffy café while old people queued up to pat her on the head and call her, 'cute'.

As she walked past an alley at the side of the cycle shop she heard a *pssst,* sound. Molly looked up just in time to see the wizard from the Magic Council appear from a cloud of mist.

'Bother,' muttered Molly under her breath. She turned on her heels and began to hurry away. Every time she met the wizard he insisted on giving her a new task.

'Molly Miggins, daughter of a witch,' said a deep voice.

Molly tried to keep walking but her feet wouldn't move. Eventually she gave up and turned back to the alleyway.

'Yes, that's me, but I don't have time for any tasks at the moment, I'm getting my learner's broom licence. Granny

Whitewand's going to teach me to fly, she's with Mum in the café and…'

The wizard held up his hand for silence.

'You will have time for this task. It shouldn't take long; no more than an hour in fact.'

Molly wasn't convinced.

'No sulking dragons? No sniffing witches? No jelly ghosts?'

'None of those things,' agreed the wizard.

'And I won't have to go to the void again?'

'Not this time. This is a nice, easy task.'

Molly looked at the scroll in the wizard's hand suspiciously. 'What do you want me to do this time?'

'The Magic Council merely requires you to go somewhere and bring someone back with you.'

Molly's suspicions were aroused again. She didn't trust the wizard. Nothing was ever easy with him. 'Where is somewhere? Who am I bringing back and why can't they come on their own?' she asked.

'So many questions,' chuckled the wizard. He held out the scroll to Molly. She took it reluctantly.

'We are about to receive a visitor from the land of Splinge, which hosts the Grey Academy. All you have to do is meet a girl called Ameera at the gateway to the Halfway House, and bring her back with you. She can't come on her own as she has to be accompanied through the portal. You will leave a package behind in the gateway when you collect her.'

Molly still wasn't convinced.

'Why me? Surely there are other witches who could do the job.'

'You were chosen for the task, Molly Miggins. It's as simple as that.'

Molly sighed. She knew it was a waste of time arguing.

'So,' she said. 'All I have to do is go through a portal and bring back a junior witch. Does she know I'm coming?'

'I did not say that she was a junior witch, but she knows you are coming and she will be at the gateway to the Halfway House waiting for you.'

Molly nodded. 'All right, I'll go and get her. When do I leave? Please don't say it's today; I have my first flying lesson.'

The wizard raised both bushy eyebrows. 'Today? No, that would indeed be short notice. You can go tomorrow. Meet me at the park gates at nine o'clock in the morning. You will find everything you need to know about the land of Splinge and the Grey Academy in your Witcher computer program.'

The wizard smiled. 'I think you'll enjoy this task, Molly Miggins, and I'm sure you'll like Ameera. Now, I'd better be off, I have important work to do.'

'Before you go, could you have a word with the people at the post office, please? They are being awkward about my flying licence.'

'Are they indeed?' said the wizard.

Molly nodded. 'The lady said that I'm too young and Granny Whitewand is too old... then she said I was too short and...'

'We'll soon see about that,' said the Wizard. 'Go back to your mother. I'll see you in a few moments.'

Before Molly could reply, the wizard vanished in a puff of purple smoke.

Chapter Three

When Molly got back to the café she found the place was full and there wasn't a spare seat to be had. She stood looking uncomfortable as old witches and some of the elderly, ordinary folk passed comment on her.

'Ooh, isn't she lovely, Hazel?' said one of Granny Whitewand's best friends.

'She's getting to be a proper little witch,' said another.

Molly hated the way people passed comment about her as though she wasn't there. She scowled and nudged her mother. 'Can we go now?' she whispered.

'Ten minutes,' said Mrs Miggins. 'Granny Whitewand's only had four cups of tea so far.'

Molly sighed and looked around for a seat.

'Come and sit with me, my dear,' said an elderly lady sitting nearby. 'I'll show you some photos of my granddaughter. She looks a bit like you.'

Molly was aghast. She didn't even like looking through old family photo albums.

The café owner took pity on Molly and produced a small stool. Molly sat down quickly; the stool was so low that she found herself at eye level with the tea pot. The effect made Molly look even smaller. It brought another round of comments from the café clientele.

'Oh, look. Doesn't she look sweet?'

An old witch called Wanda, wiped a tear from her eye. 'She looks just like me when I was a junior witch.' Wanda hobbled over to Molly and pinched her cheek between a bony finger and thumb. 'Who's a pretty 'ickle witchy girl, then?'

Molly's face went redder than the table cloth; she took off her hat, placed it on the floor and glared at the clock, willing it to move faster. She was just considering asking her wand if he knew of a *speed-up-time* spell when Granny Whitewand suddenly woke up.

'Eh, what? Who stole the fire?'

'Were not at home, Grandma.' hissed Molly. 'We're in town to get my flying licence.'

The old witch looked around, gave a jaw cracking yawn, sucked her wobbly teeth back into place, and picked up her tea cup. She took a huge noisy slurp and put it shakily back onto the saucer. 'That explains where the fire went, then,' she said. 'Has the tea shop started issuing flying licences?'

'We've got a problem with that,' said Mrs Miggins. 'The post office officials think Molly's too young to have a licence and won't issue it.'

Granny Whitewand pulled her wand from the secret pocket of her cloak and got unsteadily to her feet. 'They won't issue our Millie with a licence? We'll see about that, won't we girls?'

The old witches got to their feet and waved their wands in the air.

Molly stood on her stool and shouted to make herself heard above the shrieks and cackles.

'It's all being sorted out now; the wizard from the Magic Council has gone to the post office to have a word.'

The shrieking stopped immediately. The hags sat down and started a dozen different conversations.

'Ooh, the wizard from the Magic Council…'

'Fancy that, she must be well in if the wizard is going to get her a licence.'

'Do you think he can get me a new one? I lost mine for being cheeky to a policeman.'

Just then the door opened and the wizard stepped into the café; he walked quickly to Molly's table.

'I think you'll find that the post office is happy to issue you with your provisional flying licence, Molly Miggins. As I promised, you have been granted a special dispensation.'

The witches bowed their heads and whispered amongst themselves.

'Ooh, a dispensation, you don't see many of those.'

Molly blushed again; she hated being the centre of attention.

The wizard smiled and produced a small piece of parchment. 'You will probably need this spell to finally obtain your licence. Mr Stickitt, the postmaster, is a little indisposed at the moment. It's up to you when you use it. You can leave it until you come back from your task if you like, it would serve him right really.'

At the mention of the word, task, another dozen conversations began in the café. The wizard bowed to Molly and made his way to the door. Before he opened it he turned back and faced the clientele.

'Look after this young witch, she is very special. You may all have cause to thank her one day.'

Molly stared at her feet as a rapturous round of applause filled the room; she took hold of her mother's hand and almost dragged her out of the café.

Once they were on the pavement Molly stuck her hat on her head and sighed.

'I wish they wouldn't make such a fuss.'

'They're all pleased for you, Molly, that's all,' said Mrs Miggins. 'You didn't mention that you had been given another task.'

'I saw the wizard when I went for my walk,' said Molly. 'I don't want the task; I want to take my flying lessons.'

'I'm sure there'll be time for both,' replied Mrs Miggins. 'Now, let's go and collect this licence.'

*****

When Molly returned to the post office, she found a very different atmosphere. The counter assistant couldn't be more helpful. She bowed to Molly and introduced herself as Mrs Stamp. She had even filled in the rest of the form and all that was required to issue the licence was Granny Whitewand's signature and the signature of Mr Stickitt, the postmaster. The old witch signed it with a shaky hand, muttered, 'plastic, indeed,' and stepped back from the counter. Mrs Stamp stamped the top part of the licence and looked apologetically at Molly.

'We didn't need to do a background check after all. A gentleman from the Magic Council came in and verified all the details. Please accept out apologies and tell the wizard that your form was processed without further delay.'

The assistant looked down at the floor before continuing. 'Unfortunately, Mr Stickitt can't countersign the licence as the wizard turned him into a big, fat, slimy frog.'

Mr Stickitt leapt up onto the counter and stared through the glass at Molly. He looked down at the form he was sitting on and croaked, 'Reddit, Reddit.'

'I know you've read it, Mr Stickitt, said Mrs Stamp, but we really need you to sign it now. I don't think a wet, froggy footprint will suffice somehow.'

'Does he absolutely have to sign it?' asked Molly. 'The wizard says I have a special dustbin station.'

'A what?' said the puzzled assistant?

'A special dustbin station,' repeated Molly, 'that's what he said.'

'It's a special *dispensation*, Molly,' said Mrs Miggins. 'It means that a special arrangement has been put in place.'

'Well I've got one, whatever it is,' said Molly smugly.

'Special dispensation or not, Mr Stickitt still has to sign before the licence becomes official,' said Mrs Stamp.

Suddenly, Molly remembered the parchment that the wizard had given her.

While Mr Stickitt eyed up a couple of flies that were buzzing around the office, Molly pulled Wonky and the scrap of parchment from her pocket. She unfolded the spell and read the words closely.

'Hmm, it says this is a *kiss-frog* spell. Do you know how to use it, Wonky?'

Wonky nodded. 'I believe this is one of the old fairy tale spells that Granny Whitewand would have used when she was a very young witch. It's quite an easy one to cast.'

Molly looked round for Granny Whitewand, but she had fallen asleep with her head on a pile of public information leaflets.

Molly decided to cast the spell herself. 'How do we do it, Wonky?'

'First, Mrs Stamp has to pick up the frog.'

'Could you pick up Mr Stickitt, please?' asked Molly.

The assistant pulled a face and picked up the postmaster with both hands.

'Now she must kiss the frog while you say the words, *frog kiss*,' said Wonky.

'Kiss Mr Stickitt, please,' said Molly.

Mrs Stamp was horrified. 'I'm not going to kiss Mr Stickitt, it wouldn't be proper, I'm a married woman.'

'Well, he'll have to stay a frog forever then,' said Molly. 'It's the only way to get him back; I can't kiss him for you.' Molly shuddered at the thought.

The assistant lifted Mr Stickitt into the air, pursed her lips and pulled them away quickly.

'I can't do this, it's horrible.' She put the frog down on the form again.

'Reddit,' said Mr Stickitt.

'Bother,' said Molly, 'Oh well, I suppose we'll have to come back another day. It might be quite a while because I have a task to do and that can take ages. It could be a couple of weeks before we can get back and…'

'I'll DO IT!' shouted the assistant. 'I can't have Mr Stickitt hopping round the post office for a fortnight, what would I feed him on?'

Mr Stickitt eyed up the flies again.

Molly raised Wonky in the air and waited.

The assistant snatched up the frog, lifted him to her lips and planted a big wet kiss on his forehead. Molly aimed Wonky at Mr Stickitt and shouted. '*KISS FROG!*'

There was a flash of light, the frog disappeared and the assistant found herself nose to nose with her boss. Her lips were still pursed.

Mr Stickitt disentangled himself from the clutches of Mrs Stamp, straightened his tie, leaned forward, and signed Molly's form with a flourish. He pushed it through the counter and turned back towards his assistant. Suddenly a long, red tongue shot out of his mouth and caught one of the flies. He sucked on it, swallowed it and burped.

'Lovely,' he said and looked around for the other fly.

'He, erm, should be back to normal by tomorrow… hopefully,' said Molly. She picked up her licence, woke Granny Whitewand, and walked quickly out of the post office.

Molly rushed to the car park with her licence held tightly in her hands. As she waited for Granny Whitewand to catch up she held it high in the air and did a little happy dance.

'Look out birds; I'm on my way,' she shouted.

When they were all in the car, Molly took out the task scroll and showed it to her mother. Mrs Miggins read it carefully and passed it to Granny Whitewand.

'They must think a lot of you at the Magic Council if they keep giving you tasks like this, Molly,' she said.

Granny Whitewand read the scroll, rolled it up again and tied it with the red ribbon.

'You are lucky, Millie, I wish I could get my teeth into a nice task. Not that I can get them stuck into anything these days. Granny Whitewand sucked her teeth into place as if to prove the point.'

Molly took the scroll back and shoved it into the secret pocket of her cloak. 'You can have this task if you want it. I'd much rather go flying.'

'There'll be plenty of time for flying after the task is done,' said Mrs Miggins. 'Don't forget you get extra powers each time you finish a new task. You earned the *fly* spell years before you should have got it.'

'I know, Mum,' replied Molly. 'It's just that I don't seem to get a chance to practice many of the new spells before I'm sent off on another task.'

'This one doesn't look too difficult,' said Granny Whitewand.

'I bet it's not as easy as it appears,' said Molly grumpily. 'The wizard's tasks never are.'

‘It does seem a little odd,’ agreed Mrs Miggins. ‘I mean, any member of the Magic Council could have gone to meet this Ameera girl. I really can’t understand why they have made it into a task. People usually have to solve a puzzle or do something difficult to gain an extra witch grade. I think you’re right, Molly. It will probably be a bit harder than it appears.’

Molly sighed and leaned back in her seat.

‘Bother,’ she said.

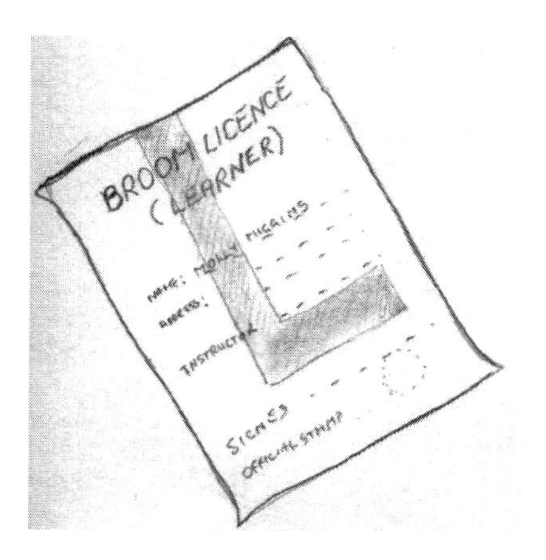

Chapter Four

When they arrived home, Molly ran to her father's study to show him her new licence.

At the side of the study door, was a tall perch on which sat a colourful parrot. The parrot had died a few years before, but it had flatly refused to cross over to the other side and remained in a sort of half-way spirit world from where he could appear at will, to do his job as a security parrot.

'Halt, who goes there?' he squawked.

'The Tooth Fairy,' said Molly, who had had many a run-in with the parrot and wasn't in the mood for his games.

'No you're not,' said the parrot. 'I know the Tooth Fairy, she's taller than you and she carries a bag of teeth around with her all the time.'

Molly sighed.

'It's me, parrot. You know exactly who I am. I've come to show my dad my new flying licence.'

'Flying licence? You're going to try to fly?' The parrot began to giggle, then he began to laugh. He laughed so much that he fell off his perch and landed in a crumpled heap on the carpet.

Molly glared at the parrot as it rolled around on the floor.

'And what is so funny about that?'

'You… haha… flying… hahaha. You don't have any wings, let alone feathers.'

'I don't need them, I'm going to fly on my broomstick,' said Molly huffily.

'Broom… hahaha…broomstick… oh my aching sides.' The parrot dissolved into fits of laughter again. 'It'll all end in disaster,' he warned.

'I'll have you know I've flown before, I have a witness.'

'Who?' asked the parrot.

'One of your relatives, actually,' said Molly. 'I met your great nephew, Polly, from the land of Splat.'

The parrot became serious all of a sudden. 'You know my great nephew, Polly?'

'I do,' said Molly. 'I gave him a lift on the back of my broom.'

'How is he?' said the parrot. 'I haven't seen him in years and years. Is he still in the security business?'

'He is,' said Molly. 'He's landed a job looking after a dragon's jewel stash.'

The parrot glowed with pride. 'I always knew he'd come to something. Have I ever told you I come from a long line of security parrots?'

'You have,' said Molly with a sigh. 'Many times.'

The parrot fluttered back to its perch and Molly turned to enter her father's study.

'Excuse me,' said the parrot. 'But where do you think you are going?'

'I've told you once,' said Molly angrily. 'I'm going to show my father my new flying licence.'

'Not without the password you aren't,' said the parrot. He fixed Molly with a stern eye.

Molly began to jump up and down on the spot.

'MILLET, MILLET, MILLET, MILLET,' she yelled.

'All right,' said the parrot. 'No need to get carried away.'

*****

After lunch, Mr and Mrs Miggins, Mrs McCraggity and Mr Gladstone, Molly's cat, stood on the patio while Molly, complete with her refurbished broom, got some last minute instructions from Granny Whitewand.

'Right, Millie, let's see how you balance yourself on the broom before we take off.' The old witch leaned her battered old hazel broomstick against the garage and watched Molly climb aboard her broom.

'Slide back a bit, nearer the twigs, you need to be able to bend the front end, you might have to avoid something big; I always seem to be having to do it these days.'

Molly bit her tongue and avoided mentioning the fact that the church tower had been on the same spot for over seven hundred years; it was Granny Whitewand's fault if it got in the way.

Eventually Granny Whitewand was satisfied and she climbed aboard her own broom.

'Last one up is a rotten egg,' she cackled. She whacked the broom with her wand, '*fly*,' she cried.

Molly had no intentions of being called a rotten egg and before the words had left Granny Whitewand's lips, she hit her own broom with Wonky and shouted, 'FLY' at the top of her voice. The broom shot along the garden path about two feet above the ground, Molly bent the front of the broom as far back as it would go and shot up above the trees before Granny Whitewand had cleared the back gate. Molly turned the handle left and circled until she saw Granny Whitewand appear above the rooftops of the neighbour's house.

'This is fun,' she cried.

Granny Whitewand caught up with Molly and signalled to her to come close. Molly slowed down and moved alongside her grandmother.

'Now, Millie, listen closely, this is very, very, important,' said the old witch.

Molly nodded, slowed her broom down to a snail's pace and leaned over so she could hear better.

'Last one to the church tower is a gooseberry,' shouted Granny Whitewand and cackling with laughter she shot off leaving Molly feeling silly and angry with herself for having fallen for such a simple trick.

Molly set off at a furious pace and spotted her grandmother as she flew over the sports field. Molly realised she could gain a bit of time if she stuck to the High Street route and whacked her broom with Wonky, 'Faster,' she cried.

Molly held on tight as the broom picked up speed. The houses underneath were a blur as she sped by. To her left she could see Granny Whitewand turn towards the shopping precinct. Molly hit the broom again and hung on for dear life. She shot over the town hall and narrowly missed a large triangular sign on a tall pole. Molly heard a siren blaring out across the sky and looked over her shoulder to discover she was being pursued by a witch wearing a glow-in-the-dark vest over her black gown; there was a yellow band around her hat. Molly slowed and the witch pulled alongside. She motioned for Molly to land on the roof of the library. Molly did as she was told and landed carefully next to a long row of parking meters. The other witch landed next to her. Molly groaned as she saw the words 'Air Traffic Warden' written on the yellow band of her witch's hat.

'Do you have a current flying licence?' asked the warden.

Molly produced her licence and the warden studied it closely.

'Hmmm, this is a learner's licence; you are required by law to be accompanied at all times.'

'I am accompanied,' said Molly. 'I'm with my grandma.'

The warden looked around. 'I don't see anyone.'

'Well she's about somewhere; we were racing to the Town Hall and...'

'You were certainly racing,' said the warden. 'Didn't you see the sign back there?'

Molly shook her head.

'It said, as if you are remotely interested, *speed restricted zone, 60mph.*' She pulled a scanner from the bag at the front of her broom. 'You were doing 70mph.'

The warden pressed a button on the scanner and a photograph of Molly appeared from a slot on the side. It showed a laughing Molly, leaning forward on her broom as it shot past the speed restriction sign. Underneath was printed the time, date and the speed she had been doing.

The warden took a book from her pocket, licked the stump of a pencil and began to write out a speeding ticket.

'Name?'

'Molly Miggins.'

'Age?'

'Nine.'

'Nine? You're too young to fly, you have to be twelve.'

'I've got a special dustbin station, I mean desperation... No, I mean...'

'Dispensation?' suggested the warden.

'That's it,' said Molly. 'I've got one of those.'

The warden shook her head, licked her pencil again, and continued the questioning.

'Flying instructor's name?'

'Granny Whitewand.'

The warden's face went pale. 'Hazel Whitewand?'

'That's her,' said Molly, 'she's my…'

'Hazel Whitewand, the serial speeder? Hazel Whitewand, the ticket dodger? Hazel Whitewand the parking meter cheater? Hazel Whitewand the witch who has caused me more trouble than every other witch in town put together?'

Molly was just about to say, *yes, that's her,* when a black shape shot across the sky above them.

'Tilly the Ticket, can't catch me,' yelled a voice that Molly instantly recognised.

The warden's face turned pink, then red, then a bright shade of crimson. She threw the speeding ticket at Molly, stuck her book back in her pocket, threw the scanner into the bag on the front of her broom, and climbed aboard.

'I'll have words with you later,' she hissed, then she hit her broom and shot off after the cheeky, speeding, broom rider.

Molly climbed back onto her broom and flew home, making sure to stay within the speed limits. She landed in the garden, stuck her broom under her arm, and walked up the path towards the house. When she reached the rhododendron bushes she heard a whispering voice.

'Pssst, Millie, is it safe to come out, has Tilly the Ticket, gone?'

Molly looked up at the sky. 'Yes, it's safe; she's nowhere to be seen.'

Granny Whitewand crawled out of the bushes dragging her broom behind her. She pulled a couple of twigs from her hair and picked up her hat from the garden path.

'Had to crash land in there to avoid her,' she explained.

'I didn't avoid her,' grumbled Molly. She pulled the speeding ticket from her pocket.

'Better you than me,' said Granny Whitewand. 'I'm already on ten points, if she had caught me today I'd be up for a six month ban.'

'But I don't want a ticket,' grumbled Molly. 'It was my first flight and…'

'Don't worry about, it,' said Granny Whitewand. 'I'll put in a word for you.'

Molly sighed and walked back to the house. She didn't think that would help somehow.

Chapter Five

After lunch, Molly went to her room to look at the new spell book that she had been awarded after completing her last task. Apart from *Fly*, which she already knew, there were a lot of other interesting spells.

Molly was particularly fascinated with the *tasty cake*, and the *change colour*, spells.

The *tasty cake* spell, if used properly, made everything on a person's plate taste like chocolate cake. Molly thought that would be especially useful at Christmas when the Brussels sprouts were served up. She wasn't too fond of celery either. The *colour change* spell would be really useful, especially when she went to parties. It meant that she would be able to wear the same clothes she wore at the last party, but because they were now a different colour, no one would ever know. She could also redecorate her room whenever she liked without actually having to decorate it.

The spell that really caught her eye though, was the *cloak of invisibility*. Molly thought it would be incredibly useful, especially if she spotted her arch enemy Henrietta Havelots heading towards her to deliver another hour-long boasting session, or for when Mrs McCraggity wanted some help with the washing up.

Molly decided to practice the new spells. She went to the kitchen, opened the crockery cupboard and selected a plain, white dinner plate that sat on a pile next to the antique, hand- painted dinner service that was only used on special occasions, and placed three "dead fly" biscuits on the table next to it. The packet claimed that Garibaldi biscuits were made with dried currants, but Molly knew that they had real dead flies and beetles in them because they tasted so bad.

Molly pulled Wonky, her ancient, slightly twisted wand from the secret pocket of her cloak and addressed it; his fat little face appeared about three quarters of the way down its length.

'Good afternoon, Molly Miggins, are we practicing new spells?'

'We are, Wonky,' said Molly. 'I've got a really exciting one to try out soon but first I want to see if the *tasty take* and *colour change* spells work.'

Molly opened the spell book, held Wonky in the air, and pointed the wand at the plate. She read the instructions carefully and called out, '*change colour, white to purple*.'

A purple flash shot from the end of the wand, skidded across the polished surface of the plate and flew into Mrs McCraggity's best china cupboard, turning all the beautifully hand painted crockery to a bright purple colour.

'Bother,' said Molly.

Molly closed the crockery cupboard and placed the Garibaldis on the shiny, purple plate.

'Right, Wonky,' she said, 'let's see if we can do anything with these disgusting, dead fly biscuits.'

Molly pointed her wand at the biscuits and called, '*dead fly...* arrgh, no, I didn't mean dead fly... STOP!.. I meant...'

A black spell shot out of Wonky and smashed into the plate of biscuits. In the blink of an eye the biscuits were transformed into a huge pile of bluebottles.

'Bother,' said Molly as Mrs McCraggity walked into the kitchen.

'Oh my goodness,' cried the housekeeper, 'I think it's time to give the food cupboards a good clean out. The flies are breeding in there.'

Mrs McCraggity picked up the plate, carried it out to the garden and tipped the bluebottles into the composter bin. When she got back to the kitchen, Molly had taken out another purple plate and covered it in biscuits.

'Where on earth are all these purple plates coming from?' asked Mrs McCraggity. 'This gets odder by the minute.'

The housekeeper snatched up the plate and tipped the Garibaldis into the kitchen bin along with the entire contents of the biscuit tin.

'You can't eat those Molly, they've gone off,' she said. 'I'll get some more when I go to the shops tomorrow. Now, get out of my way please, I need to disinfect these cupboards.'

Molly left Mrs McCraggity to it and wandered out into the hallway. *There had to be something she could practice the tasty cake spell on, somewhere.* Molly decided to see what was growing in the garden.

Mr Miggins' vegetable patch had a variety of plants in different stages of growth; Molly decided to leave the carrots and potatoes because they would have to be dug up and washed. At the bottom of the patch was a tall frame that her father had built to support his peas. Molly liked peas, especially fresh ones, so she picked two large pods and sat on the lawn to open them.

Molly split the pods and emptied them onto the grass. She addressed Wonky again and pointed him at the small, green pile. '*tasty cake, peas*,' she called.

A chocolaty-smelling, light brown mist meandered from the wand and floated across the lawn. Molly waited until it had dispersed before picking up one of the peas.

At first she thought the spell hadn't worked. The peas looked just the same as they had before, but when she popped one into her mouth she knew the spell had worked brilliantly well.

'OOOH, chocolate peas, my favourite vegetable.' Molly scooped up the rest of the pile and munched them on the way back to the house.

'This is great, Wonky,' said Molly, 'I can use this spell when we go over to Great Aunt Audrey's for Sunday lunch.' Great Aunt Audrey was the worst cook in the world; she could even burn boiled eggs. Molly was particularly unimpressed with her lumpy gravy.

Back in the house, she sat on the stairs and read about the *cloak of invisibility* spell.

She learned that she could take an ordinary length of cloth and turn it into a magic cloak that would make her invisible whenever she wore it.

Molly hunted through the house for a piece of suitable cloth, but apart from a few bath towels she couldn't find anything. Then she remembered Mrs McCraggity's work room. *There were always a few bits of cloth lying about in there.* Molly slipped into the housekeeper's room and looked around. On the table was an electric sewing machine, a paper pattern, a measuring tape and three rolls of dusky pink, silk cloth. Molly took one of the rolls and laid it out on the floor.

'Perfect,' she said. 'And Mrs McCraggity has lots to spare.'

Molly pulled Wonky from her secret pocket and addressed the wand.

'Are you sure about this? Molly Miggins,' said Wonky. 'That looks like expensive cloth to me.'

'It'll be fine… I think…' said Molly hesitantly, 'There's lots of it over there.'

Molly opened her spell book, read the instructions and aimed her wand at the silk cloth on the floor. '*Invisible cloak,*' she called.

A white mist eased from the end of her wand and drifted over the surface of the cloth. Molly slipped Wonky back into her pocket and bent down to pick up her new cloak but she couldn't see it.

'Bother,' she said. 'It's turned invisible.'

Molly scrabbled about on the floor until her hands came into contact with something soft. She grabbed the cloth and held it in the air. Within a few seconds the material became visible again. Molly opened her spell book and read on.

Once the spell has been cast, the cloak will remain visible until worn by the spell caster.

'That's perfect,' said Molly. 'I'll be able to find it when I need it.'

Molly pulled the cloth over her head and shoulders, stepped out into the hall and headed down the passage towards her father's study. As she passed Granny Whitewand's room, the door opened and her grandmother hobbled out into the passage.

'Hello, Millie,' she said.

'How can you see me?' said Molly. 'I'm invisible.'

'Most of you is,' the old witch cackled. 'Your knees and boots aren't.'

'Bother,' said Molly as she pulled she cloak away.

'Try taking your hat off,' suggested Granny Whitewand.

Molly took off her witch's hat and slipped the cloak back over her head.

'I can still see your boots,' said Granny Whitewand.

'Bother, bother, bother,' said Molly.

'You'll just have to crouch down a bit while you're walking,' said the old witch, 'or find a longer bit of cloth.'

Molly thought about going back to Mrs McCraggity's work room but decided against it. There was no guarantee that any of the other bits of cloth were any longer than the one she had used. Granny Whitewand hobbled off up the passage towards the kitchen to get an afternoon pot of tea and Molly slipped out into the garden. At the bottom, beyond the fence, Molly could see Mr Barrington from next door, working on his car. She decided to sneak up on him to see if the invisibility cloak worked outdoors.

Molly left her hat on the doorstep, bent her knees to make herself shorter, and pulled the cloak over her head. She tiptoed down the path giggling to herself.

When she got to the gate at the bottom of the garden she let herself out and crept up to her next door neighbour.

Mr Barrington was fiddling about in the engine. Molly walked around the car and stood right next to him. Mr Barrington unscrewed the oil filler cap from the engine and placed it carefully on the floor. He picked up a dirty looking oil can and stepped to the side to get just the right angle to pour the oil into his engine. As he shuffled sideways he stood on Molly's cloak. Molly moved backwards to get out of the way but the cloak slipped from her head and slid to the floor.

'AAAAARGH!' screamed Mr Barrington as Molly appeared out of nowhere.

'AAAAARGH!' screamed Molly, who was surprised by Mr Barrington's scream.

The oil can flew up into the air and came crashing down to the floor spilling its contents over Molly's cloak.

'Never do that again, Molly Miggins,' said Mr Barrington, 'you nearly gave me a heart attack.'

'Sorry,' said Molly. 'I was just testing out my new invisibility cloak.'

'You'll need to make yourself invisible when I tell your father that you've been sneaking up on people, frightening the life out of them,' said Mr Barrington, grumpily.

‘I did say sorry,’ said Molly. She bent down and picked up the dirty, oily cloak which now had one of Mr Barrington’s huge boot prints in the middle of it.

‘Bother,’ said Molly. ‘The magic might come out if I have to wash it.’

Mr Barrington picked up his oil can and pointed towards Molly’s garden.

‘Off you go before you cause any more trouble.’

Molly rolled up the cloak and stepped through the gate. She got back inside the house just in time to hear a screech coming from the kitchen.

Chapter Six

Molly tiptoed down the corridor and stopped when she reached the hallway. She eyed up the distance to the stairs and wondered if she could make it to her room before she was caught.

'What's happened to my best antique dinner service? It's turned purple.' Mrs McCraggity obviously wasn't as pleased as she could have been with the new-look crockery.

'Oh oh,' muttered Molly. She was just about to slip the cloak over her head again when Mrs McCraggity came storming out of the kitchen.

'Molly Miggins, come here, please.'

Molly walked into the hallway like a condemned man approaching the scaffold. Mrs McCraggity took Molly's left ear lobe between her finger and thumb and marched her into the kitchen.

'The excuse you are about to give had better be the best excuse in the history of brilliant excuses,' said the housekeeper. 'That,' she pointed to the pile of purple crockery, 'was our best, antique, dinner service. It *used* to have a hand-painted, meadow-flower pattern. Now everything is purple… PURPLE!'

Mrs McCraggity took a deep breath, crossed her arms, and stared at Molly.

'Out with it, Molly Miggins. What have you been up?'

'I was trying out a new spell,' said Molly, 'I didn't mean that to happen.'

Mrs McCraggity's eyes settled on the oily piece of cloth that Molly had tucked under her arm.

'What,' she said, 'is *that*?'

'It's my invisibility cloak,' Molly replied, 'but I wore it outside and Mr Barrington spilled his oil on in, then he trod on it and left a big footprint and…'

'NOOOOOO!' cried the housekeeper. 'You haven't taken… you didn't use… not the silk fabric from my work room?'

'I thought it was spare,' said Molly quietly, 'there's still a lot left.'

Mrs McCraggity slumped down on a chair and stared at the scrap of filthy, screwed up, cloth.

'That,' she said in a shaky voice, 'was part of the wedding dress I was making for my niece.'

Molly gulped.

'Will it wash out?' she asked quietly.

'No, Molly Miggins, it will not wash out. It's ruined. Do you have any idea how much that material cost?'

Molly shook her head.

'How about two years pocket money?'

Molly gulped again.

'Sorry, Mrs McCraggity, I was just practicing my new spells and I needed a bit of cloth.'

Granny Whitewand hobbled into the kitchen and took in the scene.

'Someone's in for it,' she cackled, 'glad it's not me.'

Just then, Mr and Mrs Miggins appeared at the door with a, still complaining, Mr Barrington.

Mrs Miggins crossed her arms over her chest and frowned. Molly puffed out both cheeks and let the air escape slowly. Mrs Miggins clapped her hands.

'My study… Now!'

Later that night, Molly sat up in bed reading a list of punishments that she had been given for all her recent misdeeds.

1. For turning the families antique, hand-painted, dinner service, purple. Grounded for one week.
2. For ruining Mrs McCraggity's niece's wedding dress. Grounded for two weeks.
3. For making Mr Barrington jump and making him spill his oil can. One week taken off the grounding punishment. (Mr Barrington

blocked off our garage with his car last week and refused to move it even though Mr Miggins couldn't get his own car out.)

4. For causing Mrs McCraggity to throw away all the biscuits because you turned some of them into bluebottles. Lose one week's pocket money.
5. For not tidying your room this week. One day's pot-washing.
6. For getting a speeding ticket on your broomstick. One night watching old black and white films on TV with Granny Whitewand.

Molly sighed, pinned the list on her noticeboard, switched on her computer, and loaded the Witcher program. Molly typed in The Grey Academy and sat back to read.

The Grey Academy was set up in the land of Splinge for witches who could not attend, or did not wish to leave home, to travel to the White Academy, some five hundred miles away. The Grey Academy is situated on the edge of the void and is therefore a valuable ally. The Academy leaders keep an eye on two entrances to the void, close to where the Black Academy was exiled after the Witch Wars.

Splinge is ruled over by King Milo the third. His palace is situated in the main town; Splurge.

The Splinge national dish is a strange-tasting, porridge-like meal which has been described as a cross between rice pudding and wet cement.

Splinge has a vast desert which stretches from the coast in the south to the eastern mountains rumoured to be the home of the reclusive Fire Witch.

Anyone entering the portal to Splinge will emerge at the Gatehouse of the legendary, Halfway House with its famous conundrum passageway.

Update for all visitors to Splinge.

Care should be taken when visiting Splinge. Rumours received by The Witcher, state that a breakaway witches' group is intent on making contact with Morgana, High Witch of the Black Academy. Visitors with updated information on the rumours should contact the Magic Council on their return.

Molly switched off her computer, climbed into bed, and picked up her new library book, the children's version of the Tales of the Arabian Nights. It was a book full of short stories about flying carpets, genies, princes and princesses. Molly read for thirty minutes, then turned out her bedside light. She fell asleep expecting to dream about flying carpets and genies, but instead, she dreamed of young witches on broomsticks wearing a strange logo on their cloaks, swooping down from the skies while Molly and another girl stood in the entrance of a small, dark cave.

The next morning, Molly got up so early that she had showered and eaten her breakfast before seven thirty. She put Wonky into her secret pocket alongside a map of the land of Splinge that she had printed off the night before. On impulse she picked up the invisibility cloak that had been thrown into the washing basket. Molly folded it up neatly, tied it with a length of string, and tucked it inside her tunic.

At eight thirty Mr and Mrs Miggins and Granny Whitewand got into the car to accompany Molly to the park gates where she was to meet the wizard. Before she left, Mrs McCraggity handed Molly a flask of juice and a pack of cheese sandwiches.

'Good luck, Molly,' she said with a smile. 'Don't worry about the silk. I'll get something else to make the dress out of. Your father says he'll pay for it.' Mrs McCraggity gave Molly a hug and slipped back inside the kitchen.

At nine o'clock on the dot the wizard appeared out of the usual grey mist. Molly said goodbye to her family and followed him to the far side of the park gates.

'Good luck and have a safe journey, Molly Miggins,' he said.

'Thank you,' said Molly quietly.

'Have you done your research on the land of Spinge?' asked the wizard.

'I have,' said Molly. 'I meant to ask you about that. What is that warning about in the last paragraph?'

'Nothing for you to worry about,' replied the wizard. 'I'm sure they are just rumours.'

The wizard handed Molly a heavy, brown paper parcel, tied with string.

'Here is the parcel I mentioned. Remember, this is not to be handed over until you are sure that Ameera is ready to come through the portal with you.'

Molly tucked the parcel under her arm and waited patiently for the portal to open. She looked back and waved to her family before stepping into the black hole that appeared in the hedge.

'Goodbye and good luck,' whispered the wizard. The smile disappeared from his face as he watched Molly enter the portal. 'Be very careful, Molly Miggins. Stay safe.'

Chapter Seven

Molly came out of the portal into blinding, brilliant sunshine. She pulled the brim of her hat down over her eyes and blinked a few times to get her eyes used to the light. On the other side of the portal the skies were grey and rain was expected. Molly heard a sighing noise and turned to see the portal close behind her. In its place was a high stone wall with a small but sturdy wooden door in the centre. At the top of the door was the crossed-broomstick crest of the White Academy.

Molly turned around again and re-adjusted her hat now that her eyes had become accustomed to the light. She found herself on a rough, dirt-track path leading to a series of scrub-grass sand dunes that seemed to go on forever. To her right, the stone wall continued into the distance. Twenty feet away stood a huge, stone gateway with a pair of enormous, dark-wood gates at its centre. The thick wooden planks that made up the gates were covered in pointed, metal studs; two large steel rings were set into the timber about three feet from the floor. Molly took a deep breath and smiled to herself as she tasted the salty air, in the distance she could hear the sound of waves lapping on the beach and seagulls calling. She had always loved the seaside. *I might even get to have a paddle in the sea while I'm here*, she thought.

Molly walked to the centre of the gates; put both hands on one of the huge steel-ring handles and twisted it to the right. The handle turned with a high-pitched squeak, but the doors remained closed. Molly tried the other handle with the same result. Frustrated she sat down, leaned back against the doors, and took a slip of juice from her flask.

'I just knew it wasn't going to be as easy as the wizard thought it would be,' she muttered.

Molly pulled her wand from her pocket and addressed it. Wonky's fat little face appeared about three quarters of the way down its length.

'Do you need assistance, Molly Miggins,' he asked.

'I think I do, Wonky,' Molly replied. 'I can't get these gates to open.'

Wonky thought about it for a second. 'Did we get an '*open*' spell in the second spell book you were sent by the Magic Council?'

'I can't remember seeing one, Wonky, but there might have been. I haven't tried them all out yet.'

'Just try, *Open Gates*,' said the wand. 'It might work.'

Molly pointed Wonky at the steel rings, '*Open Gates*,' she called.

A yellow spell fired out of the wand and hit the right hand ring, but the gates did not open.

Molly tried the spell on the other ring but the gates remained stubbornly closed.

'Maybe we need different spells in this land,' said Molly.

Wonky shook his head. 'Spells work anywhere,' he said. 'There is the possibility that someone has locked the gates with a special spell.'

Molly racked her brains but couldn't think of anything that might work. Then she remembered the Tales of the Arabian Nights book that she had been reading. *That might be worth a try*.

She got to her feet and spread her arms out wide. *Open Sesame*, she called.

The huge gates creaked, then groaned, as they began to separate. Thirty seconds later they were fully open and Molly could see a long, tree-lined, cobbled road that led to a single floored building with white walls and a tiled red roof.

'That must be the Halfway House,' said Molly as she stepped through the gates. 'Come on, Wonky, let's have a look. It's supposed to be a really famous building. It has a section all to itself in the Witcher.'

Wonky wasn't sure that was such a good idea.

'The wizard didn't mention going to the Halfway House,' he warned. 'Didn't he say the meeting would take place at the gatehouse?'

'You're right, Wonky,' said Molly. 'There's no one here though.'

Molly left the road and walked to the left-hand gate tower. The tower door was locked but there was an arched window that Molly could just see through if she stood on her tiptoes.

'There's no one in there, Wonky, let's try the other side.'

As she walked across the gateway Molly saw what looked like four large crows flying towards the Halfway House. When she reached the right-hand tower she tried the door, but again it was locked. Molly stood on her tiptoes and peered through the window. Inside, sitting on the floor, was a girl of about Molly's age. She was dressed in a witch's costume with a crest on her tunic that Molly had never seen before. The girl had short, brown hair and piercing, bright blue eyes. She fanned herself with her witch's hat.

Molly tapped on the window and smiled at the girl. 'Hi, I'm Molly Miggins,' she said. 'Can you open the door?'

The girl stood up and walked slowly towards the door. 'How do I know you're who you say you are?' she shouted.

'No one else would know my name, would they?' said Molly.

'That's true,' replied the girl.

Molly stood back as a bolt was drawn aside and the girl stepped out into the sunlight. 'Are you Ameera?' she asked.

'No,' replied the girl. 'I'm Lara, Ameera couldn't make it.' She looked over Molly's shoulder and shouted, 'NOW!'

Lara ran out of the tower as four witches on broomsticks swooped down from the sky. Two of them attacked Molly with *fire bolt* spells while the others came into land on the forecourt. One of them grabbed Molly's parcel. The other waited for Lara to jump on the back of her broom. Molly dived behind the gatehouse door as two more *fire bolt* spells smashed into it. She addressed Wonky and fired a *thunderbolt* spell at one of the witches. The spell smashed into her shoulder and sent her crashing to the ground. Molly turned her attention to the other flying witch and fired another *thunderbolt* spell but the girl was an experienced flyer and managed to avoid it by lying flat on her broom. She took aim again but the witch flew over the high wall to get out of the way.

Molly stood in the gatehouse with Wonky held high in the air. Her eyes scanned the sky, her heart pounded in her chest. Suddenly there was a whooshing noise from behind and the witch hurtled through the gatehouse knocking Molly to the floor. The witch skidded to a halt on the forecourt floor and screamed to her injured friend to climb aboard. A few seconds later they took off and joined their hovering companions.

Molly got to her feet and fired one last *Thunderbolt*, but her attackers were too far away and the spell just fizzled out in the air. She watched with her heart in her boots as three broomsticks, five witches and the wizard's parcel, flew off into the distance.

Chapter Eight

Molly watched the witches disappearing over the horizon and wondered what to do next. She thought about going back through the portal to tell the wizard what had happened but she hated the thought of having to tell him that not only had she been tricked, she had lost his parcel in the process.

Molly decided she wasn't going to give in that easily and walked quickly across to the broom that her attackers had left behind. Molly straightened a few twigs at the rear end, raised Wonky in the air, and brought it crashing down on the broom handle.

'*FLY!*' she cried.

The broom shot into the air and began to circle the gatehouse. Molly reached back and fiddled with the twigs until it could fly in more or less a straight line, then she pointed it in the general direction of the Halfway House and began to pursue her attackers.

Molly could just about make them out, but they were little more than dots on the horizon. She urged the broom on with threats and slaps with her wand.

'I hope there aren't any speed restrictions here, Wonky,' she muttered.

After thirty minutes, the specs had grown to egg size and after ninety minutes she could make their shapes out clearly. In the distance she could see a range of snow-topped mountains, and as she got closer she could make out four tall, grey towers, perched between the tallest of the peaks. The witches were heading straight for them. Molly gave the broom another whack and closed her targets down still further. She had almost got into spell firing range when she was spotted. Two of the witches fired *fire bolt* spells over their shoulders and Molly had to swerve to avoid them. She fired off a couple of spells of her own before she realised to her dismay that they would reach the castle before she could catch them. As Molly approached, she counted forty wand-wielding witches on the battlements. The broomsticks dropped down below the castle walls and out of site.

Molly circled looking for a safe place to land but a dozen witches took to the air and headed straight for her. She knew she couldn't fight off so many on her own so reluctantly, she turned tail and headed back to the coast.

Initially, Molly flew at full speed but after thirty minutes she looked back to see that her pursuers either couldn't keep up the pace, or had given up the chase and gone back home. Molly slowed down to a more leisurely pace and took in the landscape. Not that there was much to take in. The entire country seemed to be one large sand pit. Molly had seen pictures of deserts in her school books but none of the pictures she had seen could match the strange beauty of the place. The sun, which had been beating down all day, now dropped listlessly behind the dunes to the west of her. Molly began to think she would have to fly in complete darkness or sleep in the sand for the night, but just as she was considering landing, a pale moon rose into the eastern sky, casting an eerie white light over the dunes.

Forty minutes later Molly caught site of the sea. She followed the shoreline northward hoping to find the Halfway House and the gateway again. She had decided that it would probably be a good idea to tell the wizard about the witches with the strange logo on their tunics after all.

After following the coast for a few miles, Molly noticed an island about a hundred yards off shore. Built onto the rocks was a small but sturdy looking fortress. On the shoreline, to the west, was a largish town with an enormous building set at its centre. As Molly got closer she could see that the structure consisted of a series of different sized domes. Molly flew between the domes and looked down onto a huge square courtyard that was lit by hundreds of lamps. Molly wasn't sure if they contained gas or candles but they certainly weren't powered by electricity. She thought about the Arabian Nights book she had been reading again; the building looked just like one of the pictures of the Sultan's Palace.

The streets of the town were silent. The only movement came from what looked like a guardhouse that was situated on the main road just outside of the town. As Molly watched, two men wearing turbans came out of the guardhouse and looked up towards her. One of them aimed a spear and threw it into the air. It arced well below Molly's feet and landed on its point in the sand on the beach. Molly left the town and headed along the beach for a mile or so looking for a safe place to land. She had changed her mind about returning home until she had answers to at least some of the questions that were milling around in her head. Why hadn't Ameera been waiting for her? Why had she been attacked and who were the witches with the strange crest on their tunics? She also wanted to know more about the people who lived in the town.

Molly landed on a bare patch of scrubland about a quarter of a mile outside the town. She left the beach and headed for a pile of rocks that she thought might offer her some cover from prying eyes. She sat down with her back against a large rock, took a drink from her flask, and ate half the sandwiches that Mrs McCraggity had given her. She took off her hat, pulled out her cloak of invisibility, rolled it into a pillow, and lay down using her cloak as a blanket.

Molly stared up at the star strewn night and thought about what she should do next. She could just walk up to the guardhouse and ask them if they knew a girl called Ameera, or she could try to find a way into the town without being spotted. The wizard hadn't mentioned the palace, then again he hadn't mentioned the fact that Ameera might not be at the gatehouse. Molly thought about the parcel that had been stolen. Why were its contents so valuable? It didn't look particularly important to Molly, and it was only wrapped in brown paper and held together with string. If it held something valuable the wizard would have given her a briefcase locked with a special spell, surely. But if there was nothing important in the parcel why would the witches devise such an elaborate plan to enable them to steal it. Molly decided that it would be best to keep her visit a secret for as long as she possibly could. Tomorrow she would find a way into the town and have a look around. There might be someone there who could tell her who the witches wearing the wand and spell book crest, were

Chapter Nine

Molly awoke the next morning with the sun in her eyes. She squinted as she sat up and searched for her hat. Molly pulled the brim down low over her eyes, yawned a huge yawn and looked up and down the deserted beach. Assured that she couldn't be seen, she stripped down to her underwear and washed in the sea, there was no need for a towel, the sun had dried her face, arms and legs before she got back to the pile of rocks. Molly got dressed and ate the last of her sandwiches and had a sip of juice. The flask was almost empty now so she thought her first priority ought to be to find some fresh water.

Molly climbed over the dunes until she could get a good view of the town. The whole community was protected by a ten-foot, barbed wire fence. Molly walked carefully around the perimeter, ducking down behind the dunes every hundred or so yards but she saw no one on the other side of the fence until she reached the guardhouse.

Molly made her way back to the fence and retraced her steps. By the time she had got three-quarters of the way around the perimeter, the town had begun to wake up. The large gates to the palace were open and people walked in and out carrying baskets of fresh bread and fruit.

Molly slipped back into the dunes and made her way to the beach. On the shoreline she found a raft and a set of paddles. At the side of the raft was a large basket of coconuts. The raft was secured by a rope to a low stone wall so that it couldn't float away during the night. Molly wondered where the coconuts had come from as there wasn't a tree in sight. She assumed the residents of the town rowed out to one of the offshore islands to pick them.

All morning Molly had been watching the sky in case her attackers returned but she saw nothing other than a few birds and a single fluffy cloud. She thought about the skirmish she had been in the day before and how powerful the witches' *fire bolt* spells had been. One had taken a big chunk out of the stone wall behind her. She decided she needed to get a bit of target practice in, just in case. It had been a while since she last stood on the firing range at the Academy.

Molly sat ten of the coconuts on the wall and turned away to face the sea. She took Wonky from her secret pocket and addressed him.

'Good morning, Molly Miggins,' said the wand. 'Are we having a bit of target practice?'

‘We are, Wonky,’ replied Molly. ‘I think I need it after yesterday. I only hit one of those witches, the rest of the *thunderbolt* spells missed.’

‘The thunderbolt isn’t as accurate as the fire bolt although it’s more powerful,’ said the wand. ‘It didn’t help that I am slightly twisted, but you did well to fight them off.’

Molly turned back to face the wall of coconuts and fired off a practice *fire bolt* spell. A red flame shot out of Wonky and hit the dunes behind the wall with a *phut*, sound.

Molly took careful aim and fired off another *fire bolt*. This time it smashed into the wall just below her target. Molly adjusted her stance and fired off four quick shots hitting all four of her targets.

‘Good shooting, Molly Miggins,’ said Wonky. ‘You remembered to adjust for the twist that time.’

Molly grinned and turned back to face the sea before spinning around to fire off four rapid spells. Four more coconuts were smashed to smithereens.

‘This is great fun, Wonky,’ she cried.

‘It might be great fun for you but they are not your coconuts to smash up,’ said an angry voice.

Molly turned quickly. In front of her stood five boys, all about Molly’s age, two of them were carrying baskets, two had bows and a quiver full of arrows, the remaining, taller one, carried a sharp spear.

‘I’m sorry,’ said Molly as she slipped Wonky into the secret pocket of her cloak. ‘I didn’t realise they belonged to anyone, I was just…’

‘You were just having a bit of fun smashing up our coconuts,’ said the tall boy with the spear. He pointed it out to sea. ‘Do you know how long it takes us to collect that many?’

Molly shook her head.

‘A whole day, sometimes two, doesn’t it, Barl?’ said the boy. ‘We have to sail out for ages to find the islands with the best trees on them.’

The shorter boy called, Barl, nodded. ‘That’s right, Slem. Not that she cares; she’s just a coconut masher.’

‘Sorry,’ said Molly again. ‘I didn’t know.’

‘How do you think they got there?’ said the smallest of the boys. He opened his arms wide. ‘Can you see a coconut tree anywhere?’

Molly looked at her feet and mumbled that she couldn’t.

Slem stepped forward and took a close look at the crest on Molly's tunic.

'Careful, Shem, she might be the Fire Witch,' said the smallest boy.

'She's not the Fire Witch or we'd all be piles of cinders by now,' Shem replied. He pointed to Molly's tunic. 'That's a White Academy crest. What are you doing here, did you get lost?'

'No,' said Molly. 'I was sent here to meet someone but they didn't turn up.'

'Who were you supposed to meet?' asked the boy. He looked at Molly suspiciously.

'Her name is Ameera,' said Molly. 'I think she's a Grey Academy witch.'

'Ameera isn't an Academy witch,' said Shem. He pointed the spear at Molly. 'Come on lads, let's take her to the guardhouse, they'll know what to do with her.'

The boys made a circle around Molly and marched her along the beach until they reached the guardhouse on the main road to the town. As they approached, two soldiers wearing bright coloured turbans stepped out from the guardhouse. One had a huge curly moustache and eyebrows that almost covered his eyes. The other had a pointy beard on his fat chin and saggy cheeks that hung over his jaw.

'Well, well, what have we here?' asked the soldier with the pointy beard.

'We caught her smashing up our coconuts,' said Shem, angrily.

'She smashed them into little pieces,' added Barl.

The soldier gasped. 'Smashing up someone else's coconuts is a very serious offence,' he said. 'Do you know how long it takes these boys to collect them?'

Molly nodded. 'All day,' she said.

'That's right,' said the soldier, 'and do you realise how far out they have to go to find the trees?'

'They have to sail for ages?' guessed Molly.

'Ages,' said the guard as if he hadn't heard Molly's reply. 'You could go to gaol for five years for this.'

'FIVE YEARS!' shouted Molly. 'But it was only a few coconuts.'

‘It might only be a few coconuts to you, young witch,’ said the soldier with the droopy moustache, ‘but it’s a day’s hard work for these lads. Do you know how far they have to sail to find them?’

‘Yes, yes,’ said Molly, ‘I know that now, but I didn’t before and…’

‘Take her into the guardhouse and guard her,’ said the soldier with the pointy beard. ‘I’ll tell Ratruhn what she’s been up to. He’ll decide what to do with her.’

While the five boys stood around outside boasting to each other as though they had captured a spy, Molly sat inside the guardhouse on a low stool. The soldier with the droopy moustache introduced himself as Sergeant Sarge. His colleague, he informed Molly, was his brother, Sergeant Barge.

Sergeant Sarge was a friendly man; he offered Molly some cool water from a large jug. Molly took a big drink and filled up her flask as the boys sat down on the floor of the guardhouse.

'What do you do with the coconuts when you take them into town?' asked Molly. She wasn't really interested what they did with them but she was bored and it was the only conversation point she could think of.

'We take them to the palace and break them up for the cooks,' said Shem. 'They use a lot of coconuts, they pay us well.'

'In that case I've done you a big favour, haven't I?' said Molly.

'How do you work that out?' said Barl. 'We're going to have to sail out and find some more now.'

'Think about it,' said Molly, patiently. 'The ones you had are already smashed up so you won't need to do that bit of the job now, will you?'

'She's got a point there,' said Shem. He turned back to the beach. 'Come on lads, let's get those broken nuts.'

The boys ran off leaving Molly with Sergeant Sarge. She was just wondering whether to make a run for it or not, when his brother appeared with two other men. One, a skinny man wearing a blue smock and matching turban, carried a long, sharp sword, the other, a stockier man wearing green carried a short set of paddles.

'So, you're the coconut mangler are you?' said one of them.

'Yes, but I did the boys a favour, they won't have to smash the coconuts up now, it's already done. I saved them a lot of work,' said Molly.

'It's still a crime to smash coconuts on the beach,' said the man with the blue turban. 'People might step on a sharp bit of shell and cut their toe.'

'But no one did tread on any broken shells,' argued Molly, 'so that doesn't come into it.'

Sergeant Sarge looked at the man in the blue turban as though she had a point. The man thought about it for a moment but then shook his head.

'No, we had better take her over to the gaol like Ratruhn ordered. King Milo can decide what to do with her later… If he ever comes out of his room, that is.'

The men marched Molly down to the beach and sat her in a small white rowing boat. They pushed it into the sea, jumped aboard, took a paddle each, and began to row. Twenty minutes later they pulled the boat ashore on the fortress island and Molly was marched up a shingle path to the main gate. A teenage boy opened the steel gate and let them in.

‘Where’s the gaoler,’ asked the man in blue, ‘we’ve got a serious offender here.’

A man with a scruffy, bushy, black beard, wearing a faded, leather tunic came out of a room on the right. He was carrying a large bunch of keys.

‘A serious offender eh? She does look a bit dangerous I have to say. Have you taken her wand off her?’

‘We haven’t,’ said the man in the blue turban. It’s a waste of time looking. Witches have secret pockets, sometimes it’s in the cloak, sometimes it’s in the tunic; it can even be in their hats. You can have a look if you like but you’ll never find it. Only witches know where it is. It’s hidden to the rest of us.’

The gaoler shrugged, ‘It doesn’t matter; she won’t escape my gaol, wand or no wand. What’s she been up to anyway, Robbery? Burglary? Shouting in the streets after eight o’clock?’

‘Smashing coconuts on the beach,’ said the man in blue.

The gaoler looked shocked.

‘Come here, missy, I’ve got just the cell for you… actually we only have one useable cell these days but it was built just for dangerous criminals like you.’

He led Molly up ten flights of winding stairs and stopped, out of breath, outside a cell on the top floor. He picked the biggest key on his key ring and unlocked the door, it opened with a low groan. The gaoler pushed Molly inside.

‘You desperados can stay together,’ he said. The gaoler backed out of the room, locked the door again, and stomped off down the stairs.

Molly looked around the cell. There was an arched window at one end of the room, a small wooden table and two chairs at the side of the door and a rickety-looking bed with a straw mattress and a lumpy bundle of blankets pushed up against one of the walls. On the flagstone floor was a square of carpet with a faded pattern and curled up corners. Scratched onto the wall opposite the bed was the words, “Jazz woz ‘ere”. Next to that he had written, “for stealing the king’s horse poo”. Underneath that was a long series of marks that Jazz had scratched into the wall to show how long he had been held there. Molly counted them up. It seemed that Jazz had been a prisoner in that cell for twenty-five years. She sighed and plonked herself down on the bed. Things were going from bad to worse.

Chapter Ten

'OW! Watch where you're sitting,' cried a voice beneath Molly's bottom.

Molly screamed and leapt into the air.

When she turned around she saw a girl with shoulder length blonde hair sitting up on the bed rubbing her head.

'You shouldn't go around sitting on people like that,' she moaned.

'Sorry,' said Molly. 'I didn't know you were there. I thought this was my cell.'

'You can have it if you want,' said the girl. 'I don't want it.'

'I don't want it either, really,' said Molly. 'I'd be quite happy to let Jazz keep it. I'm Molly Miggins by the way.'

'I'm Erin,' said the girl. She looked at Molly closely. 'You're not from round here are you? What did they arrest you for?'

'Firing *fire bolt* spells at coconuts,' said Molly.

Erin shook her head. 'They arrest you for anything these days.'

Molly nodded and pointed to the opposite wall. 'Look at poor Jazz. Twenty-five years for stealing horse poo.'

'He did throw it at the king though, so I suppose he wasn't completely innocent of any crime,' said Erin.

'Ah,' said Molly. 'I can see why he was arrested.'

'He threw it at the king while he was eating his dinner. The king was covered in it from head to foot,' Erin giggled and looked towards the door of the cell. 'Be careful what you laugh at. Laughing at the king can get you ten years now.'

Molly tiptoed over to the door and looked through the metal grill.

'It's okay, no one's listening.' Molly pulled out a chair from beneath the table and sat down.

'What did you do that was so wrong, Erin?'

'I wouldn't tell them everything I knew when the king's daughter was kidnapped.'

Molly was intrigued. 'The king's daughter…'

'Princess Ameera,' said Erin. 'The Fire Witch has taken her.'

'AMEERA? That's who I was supposed to meet at the Halfway House,' said Molly.

'Is that why you're here?' asked Erin. 'I wondered what a White Academy witch was doing in Splinge.'

‘What happened to Ameera?’ said Molly, quickly. ‘Who is this Fire Witch and why did she take the princess?’

‘I can’t tell you,’ said Erin, ‘or my sister might be hurt.’

‘Who’s going to hurt them? What’s going on here, Erin? I’ll help if I can.’

‘I’ll tell you some of it,’ said Erin. ‘But not all, I can’t take the risk.’

Molly got out her flask, took a sip of water and offered it to Erin. Erin declined, pushed herself back against the wall, and lifted her legs onto the bed. Molly carried her chair over to sit beside her.

‘It all started a few weeks ago,’ Erin began, ‘when there was a big argument between the High Witches at the Grey Academy. My sister, Aspen, is a junior witch there. It ended up with Livia, one of the High Witches, locking the other High Witch in a cell. She took over the running of the place herself. Anyone who disagreed with her was locked in one of the cells in the caves under the Academy. My sister pretended to be on her side to start with, so she could let others know what was going on.'

'There are rumours on Witcher about a breakaway Academy,' said Molly. 'I read about it just before I left home.'

'It's really happened, it's not just a rumour,' said Erin. She picked up Molly's flask and took a sip. 'They bring us fresh water every morning, so don't worry about running out.'

Erin pulled her knees up beneath her chin and continued.

'My sister was keeping us updated by posting letters from the village next to the Academy but after a while they stopped the junior witches leaving the castle, so she had to sneak out at night to post the news. About a fortnight after she took over, Livia and her top witches decided that they would try to get into the void and join up with Morgana and the Black Academy, but to do that they needed a certain spell book that was held at your White Academy. At the same time as this was happening, the king received a threat that if a word of this got out, his daughter would be kidnapped. The king decided to send his daughter away and contacted the White Academy to ask if it would be possible for his daughter to join and if so, could she be escorted through the portal as soon as possible. He asked for the spell book Livia wanted, to keep her happy. Anyway, as it turned out, the day before the princess was supposed to be picked up, presumably by you, the Fire Witch appeared at the palace and took the princess away. Everyone was terrified of her, even the king. She can burn down a whole building with one quick spell if she gets angry enough. She took the girl back to her home in the mountains near the Grey Academy. No one knows if she's part of their plan or not.'

Erin paused for a while then continued.

'The same day as the princess was taken, my sister was caught sneaking out to the village and the letter she was about to send, was discovered. She was sent to the cells and we received a letter from Livia telling us that if we spoke a word of what we knew, Aspen would be handed over to Morgana. Unfortunately, someone told the king's advisor, Ratruhn, that we knew all about the princess's disappearance and he ordered our arrest. Mum and Dad are locked up in the palace and he sent me here after I refused to tell him what I knew.'

'That's awful,' said Molly. 'But it explains what happened when I came through the portal. Those witches knew I was coming, that parcel must have contained the spell book they want so badly. I've got to get it back, it's my fault they have it and if they manage to free Morgana there will be another witch war.'

The girls were silent for a while, each lost in their own thoughts, then Molly got to her feet and walked over to the window. Thirty yards below, the sea lapped gently against the rocks at the base of the fortress. Molly looked across to where the beach lay about half a mile away. She sniffed the salty air again and pulled a face.

'What's that dreadful smell?'

'That will be our dinner,' said Erin, 'they'll be serving it up soon.'

'I hope it tastes better than it smells,' said Molly.

'It doesn't,' replied Erin. 'It tastes every bit as bad as it smells.'

'They should be made to eat it themselves,' said Molly.

'They do,' said Erin, 'It's all there is. The king has declared that everyone has to eat Groo until his daughter is safely home.'

'Don't you mean, gruel?' asked Molly, 'you know, the porridgy stuff?'

'Wait until you taste it, then you'll know why we call it Groo.'

Molly returned her attention to the window.

'I wish I had a broom, we could just fly out of here,' she said.

'There are a couple downstairs, but they wouldn't be any use, they cut the handles short and there are hardly any twigs on them.'

'Bother,' said Molly. 'I was hoping we might be able to escape.'

'There's no way out of here, except through the front door,' said Erin, miserably.

'There has to be a way,' said Molly, thoughtfully, 'there always is.'

Molly looked around the room to see if there was anything they could tie together to make a rope or use to block the locks on the door but she couldn't see anything useful. Then her eyes settled on the carpet.

'I've just had a brilliant idea,' she said with a smile. 'Do you have a head for heights?'

Chapter Eleven

A few minutes later the girls heard the rattle of keys in the lock and the gaoler's assistant entered the cell. He slapped a jug of water and two bowls of pink, sickly sludge on the table.

'You two aren't going to be here much longer,' he said. 'We've just had a carrier pigeon message from the mainland.'

'Are they going to let us go?' asked Molly.

The boy laughed.

'No, but they're sending a boat for you in the morning. It seems that High Witch Livia wants to ask a few questions and Ratruhn said she can have you.'

'Why is he handing us over?' asked Molly. 'The Fire Witch has the king's daughter, not Livia.'

'Ratruhn thinks they're all in it together so he's not taking any chances. Enjoy the Groo.' The girls heard the key turn in the lock and the tramp of his feet as he walked down the stairs.

Molly picked up a bowl, sniffed at it and pulled a face.

'Is this really all you get to eat?' she asked. 'I wouldn't feed this to Mr Gladstone, my cat. I can think of a parrot I would happily feed it to, though.'

Molly dipped the tip of a wooden spoon into the sludge and licked it.

'GROO!'

'Told you,' said Erin. 'That's why it's called Groo. It's what everyone says when they taste it. You never get used to it.'

Molly shuddered. 'It's so bitter,' she said. 'Hang on… I think I can do something about this.'

Molly pulled Wonky from her secret pocket and addressed the wand. His fat little face appeared three quarters of the way down the shaft.

'Hello, Molly Miggins. Is it tea time?' he asked.

'I wish it was tea time,' said Molly 'I'd have a nice cheese sandwich and a packet of crisps and maybe a piece of Mrs McCraggity's best chocolate cake.' Molly's mouth began to drool.

'We're going to try to make this taste better, Wonky.' She held the wand in the air and pointed it at the bowl.

Tasty Cake, Groo, she called.

A wispy light brown vapour drifted out of Wonky and wafted over the bowls of Groo. When it had cleared, Molly snatched up her bowl and took in a huge mouthful.

'Mmmmm, that's heavenly,' she said.

'It looks the same,' said Erin. She sniffed at the bowl suspiciously.

'Try it,' said Molly. 'It's lovely, I promise.'

Erin scooped a tiny bit of the mixture onto her spoon and licked it.

'You're right, it's gorgeous.'

When the bowls were empty Molly took a big gulp of water from the jug and refilled her flask. 'What time does the town wake up in the mornings, Erin?' she asked.

'Some of them are up and about for about six o'clock, but most aren't out on the streets until seven.'

Molly stroked her chin, deep in thought. 'Good,' she said. 'So, you don't think the boat will arrive to pick us up before, say, seven thirty?'

'That sounds about right, they didn't come over with supplies until eight today,' replied Erin.

Molly addressed Wonky again and set an *alarm call* spell for five o'clock.

'We need to get up early, Erin, so we'd better get an early night tonight.'

'I still don't see how we can possibly escape from this place,' said Erin.

'You'll just have to take my word for it,' said Molly. She crossed her fingers and wished for success. 'We're going to fly out of here… on that bit of carpet.'

At precisely five o'clock the next morning Molly was woken by Wonky. 'It's time to get up, Molly Miggins.'

Molly climbed off the bed, yawned, stretched, and woke Erin. The girls drank some water and rinsed their hands and faces.

'It's a pity there wasn't a bit more Groo,' said Erin. 'I'm hungry.'

'We'll have to try to find some food when we land,' said Molly. 'Do you have anywhere to go? I hadn't thought about that.'

'I can go to my aunt's house,' said Erin. 'She lives a little way along the coast. My uncle is a fisherman. I'm hoping Ratruhn left them alone.'

'I'm going back to where I left the broom,' said Molly. 'I'll be less conspicuous on that when I fly to the mountains. People might mistake me for a crow or something. They might mistake me for a giant bat if they see me on the carpet.'

'Why are you going to the mountains, Molly?' Erin was horrified.

'I have to,' said Molly, 'that's where all the problems and all the answers lie. First I'll try to find out where the Fire Witch lives and if she's in league with Livia and the Academy. I can't work it out the connection, there's something wrong somewhere.'

'You're very brave, Molly Miggins,' said Erin. 'I wish I was a witch. I'd come with you, but as I'm not, I think I'd just get in the way.'

'I think I'm better off alone this time,' said Molly, 'but it would have been nice to have a bit of company for once.'

Molly lifted the carpet and gave it a good shake; bits of fluff and a few years' worth of dust flew into the air. Molly coughed as she rolled up the two sides of the carpet and pushed the front end out of the window. She climbed onto the window sill, took hold of the front corners of the carpet and motioned Erin to climb onto the sill behind her.

'Grab me round the waist and hold on for dear life,' she told the shaking Erin.

'Have you done this before, Molly?' she asked.

'No, I, erm, haven't actually, but I read about it in a story.'

'You read about it? You mean you don't even know if it will fly?'

Molly looked down at the waves crashing against the rocks below.

‘It worked in the story,’ she said, ‘and anyway, it’s the only chance we have. You can stay if you like, but I don’t think I’ll be able to fly this thing back into the room after a test flight, the window is too narrow.’

‘I want to get out of here,’ said Erin. ‘The Groo tasted lovely after you put the spell on it so I believe you can do this. Come on, let’s go.’

Molly took a deep breath, held the two front edges of the carpet in one hand, and raised Wonky in the other. She brought the wand crashing down on the carpet sending another cloud of dust into the air.

‘*FLY!*’ she cried.

Chapter Twelve

Molly and Erin pushed their feet against the stone sill and kicked themselves away from the window but instead of floating gracefully across the bay, the carpet plummeted like a sack of potatoes. The girls screamed as they hurtled towards the rocks. Molly pulled the flapping carpet from her face and gulped as the rocks loomed in front of her eyes.

'Molly, do something,' screamed Erin.

Sweating from every pore and with every hair on her body standing on end, Molly raised Wonky in the air and hit the carpet again and again.

'*FLY, FLY, FLY!*' she yelled.

Just as it seemed certain that they were about to smash into the tallest, fattest and hardest of the rocks, Molly yanked the front corners of the dusty mat towards her. The carpet, stuttered, curled into a ball, then straightened itself out flat and pulled out of the dive. The girls felt the mat scrape across the rocks as they bumped across their surface, then, amazingly, they were clear and bouncing across the waves towards the beach.

Molly took a quick look over her shoulder at Erin. Her eyes were closed; she hung onto Molly's cloak, wearing a fixed, tight grin on her face.

'Thank goodness the tide was coming in,' she said. 'If it had been going out we'd be bouncing out to sea by now.'

Molly gave the rug a few more smacks with the wand and managed to keep the carpet flying just above the white foam of the surf. Every so often a small wave caught the carpet, lifted it on its crest and carried them a little closer to the sand.

Erin tapped Molly on the back. 'Now I know what a pebble feels like when you skim it across a pond,' she said.

A few minutes later, despite Molly's desperate wand-whacks, the carpet began to sink. Molly felt her feet scrape the sand about ten yards from the beach. She let go of the mat and allowed it sink to the sea floor. Erin took Molly's hand and together they waded ashore.

'That was close,' said Molly.

'I broke one of my toenails on those rocks,' said Erin. 'I was just about to say goodbye when we pulled out of the dive.'

'It was more of a fall than a dive,' said Molly. 'It was almost a splat, in fact. That's one thing I won't be trying again in a hurry.'

There was a sloshing sound around their feet and the girls looked down to see that the carpet had washed ashore. 'I think we'd better bury this in the sand so they can't see where we landed,' said Molly.

The girls dragged the carpet over the top of the nearest dune and covered it in a thick layer of sand. Erin laughed as they went about the task.

'Imagine their faces when they bring the Groo up to the cell this morning.'

'They'll have a bit of explaining to do, that's for sure,' replied Molly. 'The gaoler said the tower was escape proof.'

After they buried the carpet Molly and Erin climbed back to the top of the dune and scanned the beach. It was still empty. The girls decided to work their way around the town's perimeter fence so they wouldn't have to pass the guardhouse or leave tell-tale footprints on the beach.

Erin told Molly what she knew of the Fire Witch as they walked.

'When we were little we used to see her quite a lot. She used to turn up at the big summer fete that we hold in the palace grounds every year. She could do some fabulous fire magic. She didn't need fireworks, she could do it all with her wand.'

'So she wasn't seen as an evil witch back then,' said Molly.

'Not at all,' replied Erin. 'No one wanted to get too close to her, she was very strange and she had this sort of red glow about her all the time, little flames licked around her cloak and hat and she left charred footprints when she walked, so nobody wanted to invite her into their house.'

'That might just have been part of the act though,' said Molly. 'I can't see her being like that all of the time, I mean to say, she has to have a bath or a shower now and again.'

Erin laughed. 'She'd be really smelly if she didn't shower, wouldn't she.'

Molly joined in the laughter. 'Especially after generating all that heat.'

Erin held her nose. 'Pe-eew.'

The girls walked along giggling to themselves for a while before Molly asked another question. 'Was that the only time you saw her?'

'No, she started to come at Christmas time too. We don't get snow here because it's mostly desert as you can see, but she used to take some of the kids away with her to the mountains to see the snow. She always bought them back again, but one or two said she had made them join in some sort of magic ceremony. They would never say what it was or why they had to join in though. Maybe she threatened to come back and get them.'

Molly grabbed Erin and pulled her down to the sand as she spotted movement on the other side of the wire. Erin peeped over the dune, a smile suddenly on her face.

'It's okay, Molly, it's Mrs Arboun, she's my mum's best friend.'

'We don't know if we can trust her,' said Molly.

'Of course we can trust her,' said Erin, 'I've known her all my life.'

Before Molly could stop her, Erin stood up and walked to the fence. Mrs Arboun stopped pegging out her washing, looked over her shoulder to make sure she wasn't being watched and hurried to the perimeter wire.

'Erin, Erin,' she whispered. 'I thought you were locked away in the tower?'

'I escaped,' said Erin proudly. 'My new friend, Molly Miggins, got me out.'

Molly lay in the sand and wished that Erin hadn't mentioned her.

Mrs Arboun looked over Erin's head and called to Molly.

'It's all right, Molly Miggins. I won't tell anyone about you and no one will ever ask. I'm just a humble washer woman; I don't know anything about anybody as far as they are concerned.'

Molly reluctantly left her hiding place and walked slowly to the fence keeping an eye out for any other movement beyond the wire.

'Ooh you're a witch, that's nice,' said Mrs Arboun.

'Molly's going to rescue the princess from the Fire Witch and then rescue my sister from the Academy,' said Erin. 'She's so brave and clever; she can even fly on a carpet.'

'Well I never,' said Mrs Arboun. 'A flying carpet, imagine that?'

'Is there any news about Mum and Dad?' asked Erin.

'They're still locked in the basement of the palace as far as I know,' said Mrs Arboun. 'The king has really taken his daughter's disappearance badly. He's locked himself in his room and won't see anyone. His chief advisor, Ratruhn, is practically running the place. I doubt the king even knows your parents have been arrested. Everything Ratruhn does is by the order of the king, so people obey him whether the order came from the king or not.'

'That's interesting,' said Molly. 'Maybe it's time someone let the king know what's going on.'

'No one can get near him,' said Mrs Arboun. She pointed towards the palace. 'That's his room up there, on the top right. He won't see anyone though; his meals are pushed through the cat flap into his room.'

Molly thought for a moment.

'I'd like to know exactly what happened when the princess was taken. She was supposed to be waiting for me at the gatehouse near the Halfway House. No one else was supposed to know she was there. I wonder who tipped those rebel witches off. It could have been this Ratruhn, fellow.'

'You can't go in there, Molly, it's too dangerous,' said Erin.

'I agree,' said Mrs Arboun. 'Ratruhn isn't a man to be messed with, if he catches you, you'll be for it.'

'I'll have a think about it while we walk,' replied Molly.

The girls said goodbye to Mrs Arboun and returned to the dunes.

*****

After half an hour's steady walk they came to the pile of rocks where Molly had spent her first night in Splinge. The broom lay untouched on the sand where Molly had left it. Erin was still unsure that Molly was doing the right thing by going into the palace.

'I'll be fine,' said Molly with more confidence than she was feeling. 'I can easily fly onto the palace roof; it's just a matter of finding my way down from there.'

'There's a balcony just outside his room,' said Erin. 'He used to stand there and wave to us sometimes.'

'That's great, Erin. I'll tell the king that your mum and dad are innocent if I get the chance.'

Erin gave Molly a hug.

'Please be careful, Molly, don't let Ratruhn catch you.'

'I'll try not to let him know I'm even there,' said Molly. 'Will you be safe from here? Do you need a lift?'

'My aunt's house is only a couple of miles up the coast,' said Erin. 'I'll be there in forty minutes or so.' She gave Molly another hug. 'Take care, and good luck.'

Molly picked up her broom and watched Erin disappear over the dunes. 'Good luck too, Erin, I'll see you soon, I hope.'

Further down the beach, the guard's boat was just setting off from the jetty. On the front seat sat a man that Molly hadn't seen before. He wore a yellow and gold turban and a finely embroidered smock. On the back seat were the two men who had paddled Molly to the fortress the night before. Molly checked her watch, it was seven o'clock exactly. She worked out that she had about twenty-five minutes before the alarm was raised.

Chapter Thirteen

Molly sat astride the broom and took the wand from her secret pocket. Wonky was unsure Molly was doing the right thing.

'The king may just hand you over to Livia at the Academy,' he warned. 'He's already promised them that he'll do that.'

'Ah, but has he?' said Molly. 'This Ratruhn fellow may have done that on the king's behalf. Anyway I really want to know what happened to Ameera that morning.'

Molly cast the *Fly* command and flew smartly into the air. She took the broom away from the guard post and flew as high as she could, hoping to be mistaken for a bird if anyone spotted her. As she flew over the palace she saw a group of guards standing by the main gates but they were busy checking anyone trying to enter with carts full of fruit and fish.

Molly flew towards the back end of the palace, away from the gates. When she thought it was safe, she dropped quickly and landed almost silently on the roof of the palace, just above the king's bedroom.

Molly lowered the broom carefully onto the balcony, clambered over the edge of the roof and hung onto the metal guttering before letting herself drop the eight feet to the floor. She landed in the crouch position and banged her chin on her knees.

'OOF!'

Molly froze to the spot, all her senses alerted. After a few seconds she straightened, picked up her broom and leaned it against the wall. She looked over the edge of the balcony for the sign of any onrushing guards, but the only person she could see was Mrs Arboun carrying a basket of laundry across the courtyard. Mrs Arboun waved, Molly put her finger to her lips and willed her not to shout out a greeting. The washerwoman nodded, placed her own finger to her lips, and carried on walking.

Molly crept up to the door of the king's bedroom and tried the handle; it was locked. She peeped in through the window but the sun's reflection was so strong that she couldn't see a thing. She decided to try to open the lock with her wand.

Molly pulled Wonky from her secret pocket and addressed the wand.

'Are we doing a spot of breaking and entering, Molly Miggins?' asked Wonky.

'Noooo,' whispered Molly. 'We're not going to break anything. We're just going to enter.'

She cast the *open* spell on the lock and pressed down the handle. This time the door opened.

Molly pushed open the door and stepped into the king's bedroom. She kept Wonky in her hand in case he was needed, and looked around the room. There was a huge four-poster bed against one wall, a couple of soft looking sofas and a row of tall wardrobes on the wall opposite the bed. Molly sidestepped an ornate coffee table and peered into the next room. The king was sitting on a large high backed chair behind a polished desk with his chin propped up in his hands. He wore a gold, jewel-encrusted crown and a red and gold robe. He looked up as Molly approached.

'What on earth are you doing in my private quarters, witch? Who let you in uninvited?'

'No one, your Majesty,' said Molly. She did a quick curtsy.

'Then what…'

'I'm Molly Miggins and I've come to help,' said Molly. 'I'm going to rescue the princess and bring her home.'

'You?' The king laughed dryly. 'How do you intend to perform this miracle? And you still haven't explained how you got in here.'

'I flew in,' said Molly, she decided to take a chance, 'from the tower that you ordered me to be locked up in.'

'I didn't order any such thing,' said the king. 'I've been in here since my daughter went missing and I'm not coming out again until she is returned. You are the only person I've spoken to since she was taken.'

'Well, someone is doing a lot of arresting in your name,' said Molly. 'Erin's mum and dad for a start, and Erin, me and goodness knows who else.'

'That's not right,' said the king, 'I haven't ordered any arrests.'

'Would the queen do it?' asked Molly.

'Definitely not,' said the king. 'She's not here anyway; she's on her way back from her mother's palace in the far west. She won't be here for days yet. I'm dreading telling her what has happened.'

'What did happen exactly?' asked Molly. 'I was supposed to meet her at the Halfway House but she never turned up.'

'So, you are the witch the White Academy sent,' said the king. 'I thought you would have gone back home by now.'

'I can't,' said Molly. 'Well, I can, but I don't want to until I get the spell book back and bring Ameera home. I feel responsible somehow.'

'It isn't your fault,' said the king. He straightened his crown, stood up and walked around the desk.

'I believe that we have been used by the Fire Witch and the rebel witches of the Academy. I don't know what their final plan is, but they appear to be well on their way to achieving it.'

The king sat down in his chair again and hung his head.

'They used us, Molly Miggins. The High Witch, Livia told me that the Academy needed the Big Book of Spells to stop Morgana and the Black Academy returning from the void. She said that the Magic Council might not send the book if they didn't believe there was a real threat, so they asked me to send a separate message saying that I was worried about Morgana's return and that I wanted to send my daughter to a place of safety. Livia told me that she would send an army of witches to destroy the town and the palace if I didn't do as they asked.'

'So you sent the message,' said Molly, 'and the rebel witches set up an ambush to steal the Big Book of Spells. It's beginning to make sense now… but what happened to Ameera?'

The king straightened up in his chair and laid both his hands on the desk.

'The night before you were due to arrive I received a visit from the Fire Witch. She told me that Livia had no intention of keeping our bargain and that she really intended to open the void with the spell book and allow Morgana to return. She said that Livia intended to take Ameera and initiate her into the Black Academy when Morgana returned. The Fire Witch said she would take Ameera to the gatehouse and hand her over to you, so that she could be kept safe. She was supposed to tell you to take the spell book back with you so that Livia couldn't get her hands on it. But instead, she sat Ameera on her broom and flew straight towards the mountains. She laughed at us as she went.'

'Have you heard anything since?' asked Molly.

'No,' said the king. 'As I told you I've been in here ever since she was kidnapped. I feel such a fool for allowing myself to be tricked like that.'

'What would the Fire Witch want with Ameera?' asked Molly.

'I really don't know,' replied the king. 'I'm assuming she intends to use her as a bargaining tool if Morgana does come back.'

'I see,' said Molly. 'But until that happens Ameera is probably safe. The Fire Witch wouldn't be silly enough to hand her over to Morgana until she has to.'

'You're right,' said the king. 'She's still in danger though.'

Molly laid Wonky on the polished table and bowed her head.

'I'll get the princess back, your Majesty, I promise, but you have to release all the people that Ratruhn has arrested. They haven't done anything wrong.'

The king came out from the behind his desk and walked briskly to the double doors at the end of his sitting room. 'Guards, inform Ratruhn that I want to see him immediately.'

'He's gone to the fortress in the bay, sire,' said one of the guards.

'Then tell him when he returns. For now I want you to release everyone he has arrested, do I make myself clear?'

'Yes, sire,' said the second guard staring hard at Molly. 'Isn't she the witch that was sent to the tower?'

Just then a canon boomed out from the roof of the fortress announcing that prisoners had escaped. 'I think they have just discovered that she is no longer there,' said the king.

Molly retrieved her broom and walked through the palace at the king's side; people bowed or curtseyed as they went. He led Molly to the great hall where he climbed onto a wooden stage and turned to address his advisers and courtiers.

'This witch,' he boomed, 'has been awarded the freedom of the land of Splinge. No one will hinder her or question her movements. As my loyal subjects you are required to assist her in any way you can. She has the protection of the king's army and the good wishes of the nation.'

The king walked Molly to the gates of the palace. Outside, people stood in silent respect. That silence was broken when Ratruhn rushed up to the gates brandishing his sword.

'There she is; the escapee. Be careful, your Highness, she is dangerous and cunning.'

'She is also the only hope we have of rescuing the princess,' said the king angrily. 'She could be on her way to achieving that goal had she not been arrested and imprisoned without my permission.'

Ratruhn hung his head. ‘I was only doing what I thought was best, Majesty.’

‘Well, you won’t be making decisions in my absence in future,’ said the king. ‘Guards, take him to the tower.’

While Ratruhn was being escorted back to the boat Molly tidied up the twigs at the back end of her broom. One of the king’s courtiers brought her some fresh fruit and a bottle of spring water in a leather bag. Molly tied it to her broom and walked away from the gates. The king smiled at her and bowed his head.

‘May good fortune protect you, Molly Miggins. The Fire Witch lives to the south-west of Castle Grey, the home of the Grey Academy. I’m sorry I can’t be of more help. I bid you a safe journey and a speedy return.’

The crowd cheered and chanted Molly’s name.

She waved and brought Wonky crashing down onto the broom. ‘*Fly*,’ she cried.

Molly tucked Wonky into her secret pocket and circled the palace. She waved a final wave to the cheering crowd, twisted the handle of her broom to the left, and headed towards the Grey Mountains.

Chapter Fourteen

Molly flew for two hours, then landed in the sand dunes to have a drink and a bite to eat. The town's people had given her some grapes, some bananas and for some reason, a couple of lemons. Molly ate some of the grapes and one banana; had a quick drink of spring water and took off again. She flew as high as she could so as not to attract attention. It was also slightly cooler away from the sand and once or twice she took off her hat to let the cool breezes flow through her hair. The sun was still strong, so after a couple of minutes she heeded the warnings that Mrs McCraggity had given her about sunburn, put her hat back on and steered her broom towards the mountains that were now looming up in front of her.

After another thirty minutes Molly could make out the Grey Castle battlements, she didn't want to take the risk of being spotted, so she turned south and flew through the mountain passes until she reached the rear of the castle which she hoped would be less heavily guarded than the front. Molly flew close to the ground looking for an entrance that she might be able to use. She spotted a small door and window at the far end of the castle wall. To her delight, the window was open, steam drifted out into the thick gorse bushes that grew up the side of the castle.

Molly had planned on looking for the Fire Witch, before trying to get into the castle to retrieve the Big Book of Spells but now that she had had more time to think about things she thought that it was probably a better idea to do things the other way round.

If she did manage to free Ameera from the clutches of the Fire Witch she would either have to take her into the castle with her, or leave her alone outside. If she got the book first she reasoned that she could leave it hidden in the mountains until she had time to retrieve it.

Molly landed on a bare patch of ground and made her way back on foot, keeping under the cover of the thick vegetation, by the time she reached the door she was out of breath and sweating heavily. She sat under the open window to get her breath. Inside she could hear the clanking of pans and the rattling of plates. Molly took a few sips of water and hid her broom in the gorse bushes, then, she pulled Wonky from her secret pocket, stood on her tiptoes and peered through the window.

The kitchen was a hive of activity. At one end, witches in cooks' aprons pulled roast chickens out of large ovens and put them onto metal trollies with plates of potatoes and jugs of gravy. At the other end, some miserable looking girls stirred cauldrons of Groo while witches wearing the rebel logo, guarded them.

'Come on, stir that Groo harder,' shouted one of the witches. 'Your friends in the dungeons must be getting hungry.'

A girl stirring the Groo looked enviously at the trolley of roast chickens and vegetables. 'It's not fair,' she said. 'We should get chicken too.'

'You could have had roast chicken every day if you had joined the rebels when we asked you,' said the witch guard. 'It's your own fault you only get Groo; it was your choice.'

The girl became grim faced and silent. She stirred the Groo with angry movements.

Molly crept to the door at the side of the window and tried the handle. The door was locked so she tried a quick *open* spell on it and smiled to herself as she heard the lock mechanism click. She twisted the handle and pushed the door open just enough for her to see inside. Molly found herself looking into a corridor with a door on the left, which obviously led to the kitchen. There was an open door at the far end of the passage which looked like it could lead into the castle itself.

Molly stepped into the corridor and closed the door quietly behind her. She crept down the passage until she reached the door to the kitchen. She peeped round the door and was relieved to see that the witch guards had their backs to her. One of the Groo stirrers did see her and her eyes opened wide when she saw the crest on Molly's cloak. Molly put her finger to her lips and tiptoed across the doorway. At the end of the passage she took a deep breath and slipped through the doorway into a large stockroom. The floor was littered with bins of flour, sugar and dried fruit. In the centre of the room was a large, stone table covered in boxes of apples and fresh vegetables. There was a double door at the far end of the stockroom. Next to it, a recess had been cut into the wall. On the floor of the recess was a wooden platform with two ropes attached to it, two other ropes hung loosely at the sides. Molly heard the sound of a squeaky trolley wheel behind her and dived for cover behind the stone table. She peeped through a gap between two wooden crates that had been piled on top.

Molly watched as two of the captive witches came out of the kitchen pushing a flat, wooden trolley containing a cauldron of Groo, They were followed by two more girls pushing a multi-shelved trolley stacked high with bowls and spoons. A few seconds later, two witch guards appeared and escorted the girls across the room to the double doors.

Molly was about to run after them when the kitchen doors burst open and half a dozen witch cooks pushed six trolleys laden with roast chicken and chocolate cakes into the store room. Molly dropped back behind the table again and watched as they headed for the recess in the wall that Molly had spotted earlier. One of the girls pushed her trolley onto the platform and pulled on the right hand rope. The platform began to rise until it was out of site. A few minutes later it reappeared empty and another girl pushed her trolley onto the platform. When all six trollies had gone, the girls walked back to the kitchen chatting amongst themselves.

'I'm so glad we've got that dumb waiter. Imagine having to carry that lot up all those flights of stairs. The food would be cold by the time we got there,' said a fair haired witch with a splodge of gravy on her chin.

'Imagine,' said another girl. 'High Witch Livia would turn us into toads if that happened. Remember Tania when the dumb waiter got stuck and she had to carry her soup up the stairs? Livia tipped the whole bowl over her head and wouldn't let her wash her hair for a week.'

The conversation faded as the girls returned to the kitchen.

Molly thought about things for a few minutes and decided that using the dumb waiter as a lift, might be a safer way of exploring the upstairs rooms than walking up the open staircase, so she scampered across the stock room and pulled on the left hand side rope. To her delight the platform came down empty.

Molly climbed onto the platform and crouched down to make herself as small as possible, then she tugged on the rope and hoisted herself up through the floors of the building. The first opening led into what looked like a conference room. There was a long oak table with a dozen or more chairs placed around it. On the wall was a big map of Splinge, Molly could clearly see the town and palace marked on it. She stepped out of the dumb waiter to get a closer look.

Molly examined the map carefully and traced her way from the coast up to the Grey Mountains. The Academy was marked with a big arrow and the words "You Are Here". A little way further across was the picture of a smaller building with the words "Fire Witch" written on it. To the south-west was a mountain marked "Snowy Peak" and just below that was a lake called "The Pool of Purity".

Molly closed her eyes and tried to commit as much of the map as she could to memory, then she returned to the dumb waiter and pulled the rope to take her to the next floor.

She crawled out of the dumb waiter into a large bedroom that had a huge king-sized bed piled up with pillows. On the cabinet next to the bed was a carafe of water, a silver plate and a book about the Witch Wars. Molly opened it at the bookmarked page and saw Morgana's evil face staring back at her. She shut the book quickly and explored the rest of the room. In the larger of two wardrobes she found a silver cloak with the words "High Witch" embroidered on it in gold thread, and a matching witch's hat with the rebel crest on it. There were also some gold slippers and a jewel covered belt.

This must be Livia's room, thought Molly.

She closed the wardrobe door and scurried across to the huge, oak door. When she opened it she found herself looking down a long, wide passageway hung with old paintings in dusty gilt frames. The corridor was so long that it needed five chandeliers to light it. About half way along the passageway stood a full suit of armour with a spear in its right hand. Closer to her on the opposite wall was a large, wooden display cabinet. Molly stepped into the corridor and closed the door quietly behind her. She had only walked a short distance when she heard the sound of voices coming from the connecting corridor at the far end. Molly panicked, she didn't have time to get back to Livia's room so she slipped behind the wall cabinet and flattened herself against the wall. A short while later she heard the voices of the guards chatting to each other about ghosts.

'I'm glad you're here with me,' said one of the guards. 'I'm sure I saw a ghost up here once.'

'There's no such thing as ghosts, Herot,' said the other, 'you imagined it.'

'I didn't imagine it at all, Rhobin,' said Herot. 'I saw it with my own eyes. It came out of the wall and walked straight down this very corridor. I was off like a shot, I can tell you.'

Rhobin laughed. 'I'll tell you what. If we see a ghost, or any weird monster or creature, tonight, I'll give you a month's pay.'

'That means I have to give you a month's pay if we don't see one,' said Herot. 'That's not fair because I didn't say I saw them every time I came up here. It was just that once.'

The guards marched straight past Molly and headed towards the door to Livia's bedroom where they would have to turn round. When they did, they couldn't help but see her.

Molly darted around to the other side of the cabinet and pulled Wonky from her secret pocket. 'What are we going to do, Wonky,' she hissed, 'they're bound to see me when they turn around.'

'Use your cloak of invisibility, Molly Miggins,' suggested Wonky.

'That's a great idea,' whispered Molly. 'I forgot I had that.'

While the two guards were arguing about who should pay what, Molly pulled out the dirty cloak from inside her tunic, threw it over her head and flattened her hat to her chest.

'What's the spell, Wonky? I've forgotten it,' whispered Molly.

'You don't need one,' said Wonky quietly. 'It works as soon as you wear it.'

'Cool,' said Molly as the guards came back down the corridor.

Molly held her breath again as the guards walked past her for the second time. One of them looked straight through her as he glanced to the left to make a point to his friend.

'So, it's one month's wages if we see a ghost, but it's only two day's pay if we don't?'

'That's right, Herot,' said Rhobin. 'You had better get ready to pay up.'

The guards walked further along the passage and Molly decided to follow them. She had only gone a few yards, however, when she felt a loose thread tickle her nose.

'AAATCHOO!'

The guards whirled around at the sound.

'AAAAAARGH!' cried Herot. 'GHOST BOOTS!'

'AAAAAARGH!' cried Rhobin. 'SNEEZY GHOST BOOTS!'

Molly looked down to see that her boots weren't covered by the cloak. 'Bother,' she said, aloud.

'TALKING SNEEZY GHOST BOOTS!' screamed Herot. The guards began to back away down the corridor.

Molly crouched down and laid her hat on top of her knees. The cloak slipped over her boots making her completely invisible.

'Phew,' said Rhobin. 'The ghost boots have gone.'

'I think we should be gone, too,' said Herot, 'they might come back.'

'No, I reckon we've seen the last of them now,' said Rhobin. 'I think they only came out to sneeze.'

Molly stifled a giggle under her cloak. She waited until the guards had turned the corner at the top of the passage before she stood up. She didn't want to risk them bumping into her when they came back, so she ran along the corridor and hid behind the suit of armour. She decided that when they passed her next time she would run up the corridor before they turned around at Livia's door.

Molly crouched and held her breath as she heard the guards' footsteps get closer. When the nervous-looking guards walked by, she got to her feet and banged her head on the spear carrying arm of the suit of armour.

'OW!' she cried.

The guards' footsteps stopped immediately, but before they could turn around, a panel in the wall opened up and Molly fell backwards through the gap. As quickly as it had opened the panel shot back into place, leaving Molly in the dark and the two guards haring down the corridor screaming about talking suits of armour and sneezing boots.

Chapter Fifteen

Molly got gingerly to her feet and cast the *glow in the dark* spell. A faint blue light radiated from her wand enabling her to see quite clearly.

She found herself in a dusty tunnel about three feet wide and eight feet high. The whole place was littered with old cobwebs that wafted about in a quiet, warm breeze. Molly wondered where the draught came from and if the tunnel led to the outside. On the wall that she had just fallen through was a short, rusty, iron lever that she assumed would open the secret panel from the inside.

Molly rested Wonky on the lever while she rolled up her cloak of invisibility and stuffed it back into her tunic. Then she began to walk up the gentle incline that she thought would take her deeper into the castle. She soon got annoyed with the cobwebs blowing into her face; her hat was covered in them and her black cloak had turned grey. 'Do we have a spell to remove them, Wonky? A vacuum cleaner spell would be good.'

'You could use a small *fire ball* spell, Molly Miggins,' replied the wand. 'That ought to clear the passage in front of us.'

Molly held up the wand and fired a short *Fire Ball*. A bright red ball of fire shot out of Wonky and sailed up the passage with a loud, echoing, whoosh.

'Bother,' said Molly. 'I hope no one heard that.'

Molly began to walk along the tunnel again. The *fire ball* had done a good job; every one of the cobwebs had been burned away. When she got to the first bend, she heard a roaring noise and looked over her shoulder to see the *fire ball* spell approaching from behind at speed.

'Duck,' shouted Wonky.

Molly threw herself onto the floor; the spell shot over her head and disappeared around the corner.

'This must be one continuous tunnel, Wonky,' she said.

'It looks like it, Molly Miggins. The spell should burn itself out shortly.'

Molly waited for the *fire ball* to make another lap of the tunnel but the spell failed to reappear, so she cast the *glow in the dark* spell again and held Wonky in the air. 'On we go,' she said.

Every now and then, Molly found a set of wooden steps pushed against the wall of the tunnel, she couldn't see the point in them at first but when she finally clambered up one of them she found a metal slide-bolt in front of her. When Molly slid it to the side, it also moved the eyes in one of the paintings on the corridor wall. Molly stared out at the figures of Herot and Rhobin who were shaking like a pair of jellies that had just been tipped out of their moulds.

Herot looked up at the painting, just as Molly blinked.

'Rhobin, you know that spooky whooshing noise we just heard?'

'Yes,' replied Rhobin, nervously.

'Well I think the ghost that made it is watching us right now.' He pointed up to the painting of the first ever Grey Academy High Witch.

Rhobin took a quick look just as Molly blinked again.

'AAAAARGH!' yelled Rhobin as he backed away from the portrait. 'It's trying to hypnotise me. The whole castle is haunted. We'd better clear off and report these ghostly goings on to Livia.'

'Good thinking,' said Herot, 'then we'll take a nice holiday, well away from this place.'

The two guards picked up their spears and slowly sidled past the High Witch's portrait.

'We're just off, your Highness,' said Rhobin.

Herot bowed as he shuffled along. 'It's not your Highness, it's your Majesty, you fool.'

The guards bowed and scraped until they got to the door at the end of the passage, then they hurled themselves through it and ran off to look for Livia.

Molly closed the eye latch and jumped down the three steps to the tunnel floor. She walked to the next lever along and pulled hard on the rusty handle, a wall panel opened with a grating sound.

Molly pulled on her cloak of invisibility, scrunched up her hat, tucked it into her tunic and walked out into the corridor as the panel groaned to a close behind her. She hurried along the passage to the door that the guards had left open; she could hear muffled voices from inside. Molly slipped through the door and made her way across a sparsely furnished room and crouched down beside an ancient wooden chest. In the adjoining room the guards were trying to persuade Livia that the castle was haunted.

'We saw them, honestly,' said Herot.

'We heard them too,' added Rhobin.

'Let me get this clear,' said a husky woman's voice that Molly assumed belonged to Livia. 'You are trying to get me to believe that you have been chased by a pair of sneezing boots and had a conversation with a talking suit of armour. Not only that, but you then confront a ghost that makes a whooshing noise and the painting of the first Grey Academy High Witch tried to hypnotise you.'

'That's more or less it,' said Rhobin. 'We didn't hang around long enough to have a proper conversation with the boots, or the armour.'

'You imagined it,' said Livia.

'No one could imagine those sneezy boots,' said Rhobin. 'They were there all right, weren't they, Herot?'

Herot nodded. 'Those boots were horrible.'

Livia got angrier.

'Look, I've got a lot to do today; I haven't got time to listen to your childish ghost stories. Now get back to work. I'm in the middle of a very important appointment.'

The two guards marched out grumbling to themselves. They checked that it was safe to go into the corridor twice before they finally plucked up the courage to leave the safety of the doorway.

As soon as they had gone, Molly slipped into the ante room and followed Livia through another set of doors to a huge, open assembly hall. A large statue of the Academy's founder stood overlooking rows and rows of wooden pews that ran the full length of the chamber. In front of the statue was a tall wooden lectern. An old witch with a haggard face and a long thin chin stood next to it. Small flames licked around her black hat and cloak. Her eyes glowed like hot embers as she turned to watch Livia approach.

'I trust that was something important?' she said in a crackly voice.

'Something and nothing,' replied Livia. 'Now, where were we?'

'You were about to show me the Big Book of Spells.' The Fire Witch licked her lips and a tiny red flame flickered along the edge of her tongue.

'Ah, yes, that's right,' said Livia. She walked to the lectern and pressed a hidden switch. The lectern slid forward and Livia pulled out an ancient, thick book from a secret cavity underneath. She placed the book on the lectern and flicked through the pages until she found the one she wanted. 'Behold!' she cried. 'Here is the spell of *seeing*. When I cast this spell we will be able to see into the void and actually speak to Morgana.'

The Fire Witch smiled a fiery smile. 'And what of the other spell you spoke about?'

Livia turned the pages of the Big Book of Spells until she found the spell she wanted. 'Here is the *unseal* spell. With this we can open the void and allow Morgana to return to our world. Imagine the power the three of us will hold. We will smash the White Academy and take control of the Magic Council. In a few short weeks we could rule the whole of witch-kind.'

The Fire Witch hobbled towards the lectern. 'I'm not sure we can trust Morgana, I mean, look what she did last time. She never was one to share power. She likes to keep it to herself.'

'She'll share with us, I'll demand her promise before we unseal the void,' said Livia.

'Do you really think she will keep her word?' asked the Fire Witch. 'I'm not really interested in ruling witch-kind. I'll be happy just ruling Splinge. I'd like to cut a deal with her about that. She'll need my help if she's ever to get though the portal, witch's army or not. I have the king's daughter and he won't even think about warning the Magic Council while she is my prisoner.'

'I'm sure you will be able to come to some sort of arrangement with her,' said Livia. 'Now, come, let's invoke the first spell.'

Molly crawled along the row of pews on her hands and knees and sat down on the first row with her knees tucked up under her chin so that she was completely covered by the cloak of invisibility.

Livia pulled an elegant, silver wand from her secret pocket and held it above her head. She pointed it at the stone wall behind the statue of the Academy's founder and read out the words from the book. Livia clapped excitedly and the Fire Witch held her breath as a thick mist crept out of the cracks in the wall. Molly left the row of pews and crawled forward another few feet to get a better look.

As the mist began to clear Molly found that she could see straight through the stone wall. On the other side, a crowd of witches jumped up and down excitedly. Their voices fell silent as a dark figure moved between them. The witches bowed and mumbled Morgana's name. In the blink of an eye she was there, at the wall, wearing a thin smile on her blue lips. Her face looked really old but had no wrinkles; her eyes were black as coal. She wore a black hat and a simple black tunic and cloak with the emblem of the Black Academy emblazoned on her chest. When she spoke, her voice sounded almost melodic.

'Good day, Livia, my servant. How goes our plan?'

'The plan goes well, Majesty,' Livia curtseyed.

'Introduce me to your companion,' said Morgana. 'I have been alone for such a long time, new faces are such a luxury.'

The Fire Witch stepped forward. 'Morgana, I am Sholeh, the Fire Witch. I have a plan that you might find interesting, I'm hoping we can come to an arrangement that is advantageous to both of us.'

Morgana's black eyes lit up with a piercing green light as she held the Fire Witch under her gaze. Sholeh tried to pull away but Morgana was too strong. Eventually she turned back to Livia leaving the Fire Witch looking drained and shaken.

'All is clear to me,' she said. 'The Fire Witch wishes to strike a bargain using the king's daughter as collateral. I am not inclined towards such an agreement. I see everything, Sholeh, I know where you are keeping this child and I know that I can drive a far harder bargain with her father than you could ever dream of. Now, bow to my majesty and be silent.'

The Fire Witch fell to her knees and remained still, afraid to move a muscle.

Livia walked back to the lectern and turned the pages until she found the spell to unseal the void. Then she stood still, waiting for a signal from Morgana as the shadowy crowd of witches began an ancient chant. Molly shuffled back to the pews and pulled Wonky from her secret pocket.

'What are we going to do, Wonky?' she whispered. 'She's going to let Morgana out of the void.'

'We have to stop her, Molly Miggins, we can't let this happen.'

'I agree, Wonky, but how?'

Wonky smiled. 'I know every spell in the Big Book of Spells, Molly Miggins. I was the first wand to use many of them. I helped compile that book and what's more, I know what order the spells are listed in. What if Livia was to read out the *seal* spell instead of the *unseal,* spell?'

'How do we get her to do that, Wonky? Won't she be aware that she is reading the wrong spell?' asked Molly.

'I don't think she will,' said Wonky. 'The *seal* and *unseal* spells are very similar and more importantly, they aren't written in plain English, so she may not understand exactly what she is saying. The best thing is, the *seal* spell is on the very next page, we just need to flick it over somehow.'

'That's a great plan, Wonky,' whispered Molly, 'but how are we going to distract her while I turn the page?'

'We need a little diversion,' said Wonky. 'As I told you, I know all of the spells in that book. One of them is an illusion spell. Use the spell *seachmall,* with whatever words you want to make the illusion about.'

Molly nodded. 'I understand, Wonky. What if I was to magic up a couple of guards? That might do it, she's angry with them already.'

Molly pointed her wand to the doors at the back of the assembly room and whispered the command, *Seachmall Castle Guards.* A light, almost invisible mist drifted out of Wonky and floated across the hall to the rear door. A few seconds later, two guards, not dissimilar to Rhobin and Herot appeared and stamped to attention in unison.

Livia turned quickly to see who had the temerity to disturb her. Her face turned crimson with rage when she saw the guards. She stormed away from the lectern still brandishing her wand and marched to the back of the hall.

Molly rushed to the lectern as quickly as her crouched position allowed her to. She reached up, turned the thick page, and squatted at the side of the lectern with her chin tucked tightly over her pulled-up knees. Livia returned looking puzzled, mumbling something about needing to get a pair of spectacles. The chanting witches became silent. The Fire Witch kept her eyes on the floor, too frightened to move. Suddenly the temperature dropped and the air became icy cold. Molly pulled her invisibility cloak tightly around her. Livia gasped as Morgana's face appeared floating above the lectern. The cruel face narrowed its eyes and nodded to Livia. The witches began to chant again.

Molly crossed her fingers and wished with every ounce of her being that the trick would work. She knew that if the void was unsealed it would mean another witch war, and this time she would be right in the middle of it.

Livia raised her wand and pointed it towards the crowd of witches. A smile crossed her face as she read the ancient script from the Big Book of Spells.

Dhúnadh buan

Morgana's face contorted with rage as Livia's words echoed around the room.

'Fool,' she cried.

Before Livia could respond, the wall began to solidify. The Fire Witch fell backwards and rolled over with surprising agility as a giant, three-ton slab of rock appeared out of thin air and crashed onto the ground in front of the screaming witches. Another slab quickly followed, then another and another until the new wall touched the ceiling. A few seconds later, a milky, liquid oozed through the wall until all the cracks and joints were sealed. Then silence descended.

'Well, you certainly made a mess of that one,' cackled the Fire Witch. 'I wouldn't want to be in your cloak when Morgana catches up with you.'

'This cannot be,' screamed Livia. She dropped her wand and picked up the Big Book of Spells. She read the spell to herself, then flipped back to the previous page, a look of horror came over her face as she realised what had gone wrong.

'I've sealed it forever,' she whispered. She began to walk back and forth trying to work out how it could possibly have happened. Eventually her eyes rested on the Fire Witch.

'Don't look at me, dear, I was in over there by the wall.'

The rebel High Witch fell to her knees as the incensed face of Morgana reappeared in front of the newly built wall. Her eyes were like narrow slits, she glared at Livia.

'A young witch from the White Academy did this… FIND HER!' she commanded.

'Yes, Mistress,' cried Livia. She ran up and down the rows of pews frantically searching for the intruder.

Molly doubled up into the tiniest shape she could manage and addressed Wonky in case she had to fight her way out. Livia ran out of the assembly hall screaming at the top of her voice.

'FIND THE INDTRUDER WITCH. BRING HER TO ME!'

The Fire Witch shuffled slowly down the hall, when she reached the first row of pews she stopped as if she sensed something.

'I know you are hiding here,' she croaked. 'That was a very brave, if stupid, thing to do.' She looked back at the irate face of Morgana that, although slowly fading, still hung above the lectern. 'I'll leave you to reap the consequences of your actions. Good day.'

Molly watched the Fire Witch leave the assembly hall and waited another five minutes before daring to move. She kept the pews between her and the door and crawled the full length of the room under her cloak of invisibility. By the time she reached the ante room, the Fire Witch had gone. Molly stepped out into the passageway and raced back towards the corridor outside Livia's room.

If I can get to the secret passage, I'll be safe, she thought.

As Molly reached the final turn in the corridor she tripped and fell headlong. She picked herself up and reached for her cloak of invisibility which had slipped off during her fall. As she bent to pick up the cloak she heard the sound of running feet and calls of 'There she is.' She looked back over her shoulder to see a large group of witches running along the passageway towards her. Molly breathed in a deep lungful of air and ran for her life.

Chapter Sixteen

Molly hurtled down the corridor with the gang of witches hot in pursuit. She looked over her shoulder as she approached the suit of armour, her mind racing. The leading witches hadn't yet reached the corner of the passage. Molly pulled up the spear arm of the armour to open the secret passage, but instead of diving into it, she ran on to Livia's bedroom. She threw herself inside, slammed the door and fired a *triple lock* spell at it. Molly pulled the key out of the lock and put her eye to the keyhole. The rebel witches had stopped by the suit of armour and appeared to be arguing amongst themselves as to who should be the first to enter the secret passage. No one seemed to want the honour. Molly punched the air, her trick had worked. She ran to the dumb waiter and lowered herself to the kitchen level.

Molly leapt from the dumb waiter platform onto the cold flagstones and aimed a *fire bolt* spell at the pulley rope. The rope burned through in an instant. She smiled to herself. The rebels wouldn't be able to follow her down the dumb waiter even if they did manage to break the triple lock on Livia's door.

Molly crept across the storeroom thinking about what she ought to do next. Somehow she had to find a way to release all of the prisoners from the dungeon of the castle. She had a quick look into the kitchen and saw twelve Grey Academy witches washing pots in a row of sinks while ten rebel witches watched over them. Molly slipped past the kitchen and opened the door that led outside. She pulled out her invisibility cloak, walked slowly back to the kitchen door and waited until one of the Academy witches turned towards her, then she held a finger to her lips and mouthed, 'get ready.'

The witch nodded, nudged the witch next to her and flicked her head towards the door.

Molly stood in the doorway, took a deep breath and shouted.

'Down with the rebels. Boooooo.'

Twenty-two faces turned in an instant towards the door. Molly stuck out her tongue and blew a huge raspberry. The rebel witches' faces grew angry. Molly backed away from the door, thumbed her nose and blew another raspberry.

'Can't catch me,' she cried.

The rebel witches hurried across the kitchen.

Molly backed off to the far wall and covered herself in her invisibility cloak. The witches hurtled past her shouting as they ran.

'Get her!'
'We'll teach her to blow raspberries.'
'She's gone outside, hurry.'
When the last of the witches were outside, Molly tore off her cloak and slammed the heavy oak door shut. She pulled out her wand, cast a *triple lock* spell on the door, and shouted to the girls in the kitchen.
'Quick, get anything heavy and pile it in front of the door.'
The girls dragged tables and chairs from the kitchen and piled them up in the corridor. Molly caught hold of the sleeve of one of the girls as she carried a chair into the passage.
'Close the kitchen windows,' she ordered. 'Don't let them back in.'
The girl ran back into the kitchen and slammed the thick glass windows shut in the faces of the rebel witches. When the last window was closed she joined the group of excited girls in the store room. Molly took her to one side. 'What's your name?' she asked.
'I'm Aspen,' said the girl.
'I'm Molly Miggins and I've come to rescue you,' said Molly with a smile. 'I met your sister, Erin.'
Aspen jumped up and down excitedly. 'What can we do to help?'
'Firstly,' said Molly. 'I need to know how long it will take those witches to find their way round to the front of the castle.'
'At least a few hours,' said Aspen. 'The castle is built into the rocks at both ends, the only way round is to take the path through the mountains. They won't get there until late tonight.'
'Brilliant,' said Molly. 'Now, we all need to be very quiet,' she put her finger to her lips. 'I need to know about the dungeons. Are they heavily guarded?'
'There are only two guards down there,' replied Aspen. 'I know because I have to take them food when we feed the prisoners.'
'How many prisoners are there?' asked Molly.
'About two hundred including the High Witch and the staff,' said Aspen. 'There are about thirty big cells down there and they're all pretty full.'
'How many rebels are there do you think?' asked Molly.
'About sixty not counting the ones you just locked out,' said Aspen, 'but a lot of them don't really want to be rebels. Livia threatened to hurt their families if they didn't join.'

'Right', said Molly firmly, 'show me the way to the dungeons.'

*****

Molly followed the group of excited witches through the doors of the storeroom into a large entrance hall. The hall walls were littered with paintings of famous witches and wizards. There was a row of high, arched, stained glass windows that ran the full length of the room and an enormous silver chandelier hanging from the ceiling. Below the centre window was a pair of double doors that were held together with a sturdy wooden bar. Opposite the door was a wide marble staircase that led up into the Academy. At the side of the staircase was a huge pile of broomsticks. Molly could hear a lot of noise coming from the upper floors as the search for her went on. The girls ran across the open space to a door at the right hand corner of the entrance hall. Aspen opened it and waited for Molly to step through.

Inside, a winding stair led to a dimly lit basement. Molly tiptoed down the stair with Wonky in her hand. The girls followed, trying to be as quiet as they could.

The staircase led her into a damp, musty smelling cellar which had casks of wine laid out in racks along the floor. Aspen tapped Molly on the shoulder and pointed to the opening of a torch-lit, passageway. She tiptoed across the cellar and peered into the gloom. Molly could hear the muffled voices of two men and the odd whispered conversation of the Grey Academy witches in their cells. She sneaked down the corridor to the guard room. Inside two men were drinking steaming, hot tea out of tin mugs.

'I don't believe a word of it myself,' said one of the men.

'I don't know so much, Rolf,' said the other, 'I've seen some strange things when I've been down here on my own at night.'

'That's because you pinch the wine, Jammer,' said Rolf. 'You should do what I do and stick to tea, you don't see strange things then. A pair of sneezy, ghost boots wouldn't scare me anyway.'

'I'm scared of sneezy, ghost boots just thinking about them,' said Jammer.

Molly grinned and pulled out her invisibility cloak. She dropped it over her head and stepped into the guardroom.

Jammer was first to spot the boots. He stood up and edged his way around the table.

'B b b boots,' he whispered. 'The g g g, ghostly boots are here. Run!'

Rolf leapt to his feet spilling hot tea down the front of his trousers. He slapped at his legs as he hopped around the room.

'AAAAGH, that's hot... aaaaargh, the boots... Don't come any closer, I'm going, I'm going.' Rolf backed out of the room and ran after Jammer.

'Help, help, the ghostly boots, are here,' screamed Jammer. The guards ran for the stairs hardly noticing the girls in the wine cellar.

Molly picked up six steel rings of keys and ran out into the corridor. She passed them to the girls and ordered them to open up the cells while she had a look in the rooms further along the passageway. The walls of the first room were covered in pigeonholes, laid out in alphabetical order. Each individual hole contained a wand and a card with the name of its owner written on it. The floor in the next room was piled high with cloaks, tunics and hats. Molly stepped back into the corridor just as the High Witch was released from her cell. She approached Molly and bowed.

'I do not know how to thank you, Molly Miggins,' she said. 'I'm the High Witch Sylvia.'

'There's no need to thank me,' said Molly, 'anyway, the job's not done yet.'

The corridor filled up rapidly with freed witches, Molly pointed to the rooms she had just discovered. 'Hurry,' she said. 'Grab your wands and cloaks; I think you're going to need them very soon.'

While the witches sorted out their wands, Molly and Aspen ran back up the winding staircase and out into the hall. The noise upstairs had become a crescendo. Molly crossed the hall to the main entrance of the castle. The front doors had been thrown wide open; the thick locking bar lay on the floor. She stepped outside and saw four guards running as fast as their legs could carry them down the cobbled drive. Molly stood outside for a few moments and looked at the front of the castle while she decided what to do next. Suddenly she had an idea. She ran back inside and dragged Aspen into one of the rooms that came off the entrance hall. It turned out to be the library.

'Aspen,' she said quickly. 'I need you to open the two big windows up there. When you see me fly through, close them again as quick as you can.'

Molly ran to the pile of broomsticks by the side of the staircase and selected a sturdy broom, she patted one or two twigs into place and walked back to stand in the centre of the hallway. A few moments later, the rebel witches began to pour down the stairs.

'There she is,' shouted a dark-haired witch. 'Come on, girls, get her.'

Molly blew a raspberry at them and sat astride the broom. She held her position as the rebels hurtled across the hall, when the lead witches were six feet away, Molly hit the broom with her wand and cried *rise*.

As the broom rose, the witches jumped and flailed their arms in the air in a desperate attempt to catch her. 'Do I have access to a protection spell, Wonky,' Molly asked.

'You do, Molly Miggins,' said the wand, 'just call *protect.*'

Molly held her wand above her head, aimed it down at herself and called *protect*. An orange mist eased out of Wonky and enveloped her body.

Molly flew up to the celling and circled the huge chandelier. *Fire bolt* spells bounced off her and deflected around the room.

Many of the witches had to duck to avoid their own spells as they rebounded back at them.

'Can't catch me,' cried Molly as she headed for the open doors.

The witches stopped firing and ran for their brooms, Molly hovered in the doorway blowing raspberries and thumbing her nose. When the first of the rebels launched her broom Molly shot through the doors and made a sharp right hand turn. She flew through the library windows before the leading witch had even reached the front door. Aspen slammed the windows shut as Molly jumped off her broom and ran to the library door. The girls gave a high five as the last of the rebels flew out into the early evening darkness. Molly and Aspen closed the great doors and lifted the locking bar into place. Molly waved towards the cellar door and Sylvia and the now dominant force of witches came out of the dungeons, into the hall.

Chapter Seventeen

Silvia led Molly and the Grey Academy witches up the ornate, red carpeted staircase to a landing on the first floor. She turned left and they climbed two more flights before joining the long, wide corridor that led to the assembly room. They hadn't seen a single rebel witch since she had shut the door on the chasing pack in the hallway.

Silvia took out her wand as she walked into the assembly room with Millicent, the head of witchcraft by her side. Molly and Aspen walked behind followed by the long line of Academy witches.

They found Livia at the lectern turning pages of the Big Book of Spells in a desperate attempt to find something she could use to restore Morgana's faith in her. The twenty or so rebel witches that remained in the castle stood around looking nervous. Morgana's dark, malevolent; apparition had faded to little more than a grey wispy cloud.

'Livia,' called Sylvia, 'The time has come to pay for your misdeeds.'

Livia stopped flicking through the pages and turned round to face her accusers.

'You have no power over me, Sylvia. I am of equal rank, I make my own decisions.'

'Not anymore,' said Sylvia. She raised her wand and cast a *freeze* spell. Livia cast a *protect* spell and fired a *fire bolt at* Sylvia. Sylvia cast a *deflect* spell and raised her wand to fire again. The two witches stood face to face, each waiting for the other to make a move. The silence lasted a full two minutes. It was broken by Morgana.

'Livia, you have failed me. I cast you out. You are not worthy of the Black Academy.'

Livia's lip began to tremble. 'Please, don't cast me out. I did my best, I got the spell book for you, I took over the Academy and I fooled the Magic Council. It wasn't my fault, please…'

Livia dropped to her knees and began to beg, Morgana looked on scornfully. Sylvia walked forward and took the wand from Livia's limp hand. She slipped it into her pocket and placed her own wand on Livia's shoulder.

'Livia. You have betrayed the Magic Council. You have used your powers to do evil things. You are hereby expelled from our order. I strip you of your power and rank. You are no longer a witch.'

A ghostly, grey shape rose up from Livia's crouched form; it bowed to the assembled witches and hovered above Sylvia's wand. Sylvia bowed to the ghostly form and muttered the words, 'I release you.' The magical spirit disappeared in an instant, leaving no trace.

Sylvia turned her attention to the rebel witches.

'I know that some of you were threatened or beaten until you submitted to Livia's will. I also know that some of you willingly took her side against us, hoping to profit from her traitorous acts. I now give you a choice. Return to the Academy or leave us forever.'

Sixteen of the witches crossed the floor to stand in front of Sylvia. One of them had her arm in a sling; she looked at Molly and lowered her eyes. 'I'm so sorry; she forced us to attack you. We didn't want to really.'

'Oh, shut up, Cyneth,' hissed one of the witches who had refused Sylvia's offer. 'You were happy to attack her. In fact, I'm sure it was your idea.'

'It wasn't, honestly,' the girl turned to Molly. 'Please believe me, I really am sorry.'

Molly smiled and stepped from behind Sylvia to give the young witch a hug. Morgana's eyes settled on her.

'So, here is the junior witch that caused us so much trouble.' Her eyes turned black as she stared at Molly.

Molly felt Morgana slip into her mind trying to read her thoughts. She tried to think of something, anything that would keep her probing questions at bay. She thought about her cat, Mr Gladstone and the security parrot, suddenly Granny Whitewand's face appeared in her head.

'Hello, Millie, what are you doing in my dream,' she said.

I'm in trouble Granny Whitewand. Morgana is in my head.

Well, get her out, Millie, she shouldn't be there. Bye now, got to go; I'm in this really good dream with Penny Pimple…' As quickly as she had appeared, Granny Whitewand left Molly's thoughts.

'So, Millie… No, *MOLLY* Miggins, you are discovered. Come forward; talk with me for a while. I have room in my Black Academy for promising young witches like you.' Morgana's voice was as sweet as honey. A radiant smile lit up her face.

'I'll never join you,' said Molly. 'EVER.'

Morgana scowled. 'So be it, young witch, but hear this. The next time we meet things will not go well for you. This… creature,' she looked down at the still grovelling Livia, 'allowed you to get the better of her and, therefore, the better of me. This will *never* happen again, so savour your victory, Molly Miggins, it will be your last.'

'I'm not frightened of you,' said Molly with more confidence than she felt. 'I'll beat you again, and again, you see if I don't.'

The assembly room echoed with the sound of Morgana's laughter.

'You will beat me again? You, a level one witch with a first grade wand? I think not. Now get out of my sight before I get really angry.'

Molly stuck out her chin and pulled Wonky from her secret pocket.

'I may be young, but I'm not a level one witch and I certainly don't have a first grade wand.' She held Wonky high in the air. 'You have met before, I believe.'

Morgana's eyes rested on Molly's wand. 'It can't be… CEDRON… you were destroyed at the final battle.'

'I was damaged, almost beyond repair,' replied Wonky, 'but I was not destroyed. It took many hundreds of years, but I healed and I am back. I have a new name but I am still the same Cedron that defeated you all those years ago. I have a new owner now and while she is still learning, she has it in her to be the most powerful witch the world has ever seen. So, Morgana, it should be you who has concern for her future, not Molly Miggins. I advise you to stay where you are, because should you ever leave the void you will find us waiting, and we will not be gentle.'

Morgana's voice lost some of its confidence.

'So, you have a new hand to wield you, Cedron, or Wonky, whatever you call yourself now. But this young novice will never beat the Black Witch in combat. You were lucky last time, and I have suffered many long years because of that. This time I will have my revenge, I will prevail.'

Morgana's eyes fell upon Molly again. 'Run, young witch, before I turn you into a worm and feed you to my pet raven.'

'Use the spell, *cease illusion*, Molly Miggins, that ought to shut her up,' said the wand.

Molly pointed Wonky at the wispy apparition and called up the *cease illusion* spell. Morgana's face shrank until it was the size of an onion, then it disappeared with a pop, leaving the hall in silence.

Molly slipped Wonky into her secret pocket while Sylvia and Matilda stripped the remaining rebel witches of their wands and powers. Sylvia picked a dozen Grey witches to escort them to the dungeons.

Over the next few hours, all of the remaining rebel witches turned up at the front gates. They were questioned and given the chance to re-join the Academy. All but one agreed.

Molly slept like a log that night and woke up refreshed and ready to face the final part of the task she had set herself. She had a big breakfast, filled up her flask and walked down the main stairway to the big double doors in the hall. Sylvia and Aspen walked with her to see her off.

'Are you sure you don't want an escort, Molly Miggins, we will happily provide one.'

'No, thank you,' said Molly. 'This is something I have to do myself.'

Sylvia laid her hand on Molly's arm. 'The Book of Big Spells is locked away in my office. I will give it to you on your return, though I must admit it would be nice to have such a treasure in our library.'

'I think I'd better take it back with me,' said Molly, 'but I'll tell the wizard what you said, he might send a copy of the book as a reward.'

Aspen gave Molly a hug.

'Hurry back, Molly Miggins, High Witch Sylvia has given me permission to return home for a holiday. I'd love to fly back with you if you don't mind.'

'I'd like that,' said Molly, 'but for now, goodbye. I'll see you when I return.'

She sat astride her broom and gave it a whack. '*FLY*,' she cried.

Molly circled the castle while she worked out her exact position, then she pointed her broom to the south-west and headed towards the Grey Mountains and the home of the Fire Witch.

Chapter Eighteen

Molly closed her eyes as she flew and tried to remember the details of the map she had seen on the wall in Castle Grey, but the events of the previous day had made her memory a little sketchy.

She flew down the full length of the Western side of the mountain range until she saw the desert looming up in front of her, then she turned around and flew along the Eastern side. After an hour's flying, she saw a plume of light-grey smoke drift out from between two sharp peaks. She dropped lower to investigate and saw a sturdy stone house with a dark grey tiled roof, nestled in a narrow gully. The house looked to be on two levels but it had no windows at all. The stone that had been used to build the house was the exact same colour as the mountain rock; Molly thought how easy it would be to fly straight over the top without noticing it.

She found an area of rough, but flattish ground to land on and trod carefully over the sharp edged rocks that lay sprawled across the front of the house like a grey lawn.

Molly walked all the way around the grey house but there didn't appear to be an entrance of any kind. *No doors, no windows, how does she get in and out?* She decided to ask Wonky who was good at spotting illusions and cover up spells.

Molly pulled Wonky from her secret pocket and addressed the wand.

'Hello, Molly Miggins, can't you find a way in?'

'I can't, Wonky, it's made of solid stone, there aren't any doors or windows.'

'A spell has been cast on this building, Molly Miggins. If you use the *cease illusion* spell again, you might have a pleasant surprise, but beware, all may not be as it seems.'

Molly pointed Wonky at the dull grey building and called, *cease illusion*. In an instant the house was transformed. Gone was the dull, grey featureless building and in its place sat a cottage that looked very similar to the one that Molly's Aunt Matilda lived in. The sharp rocks at the front of the house suddenly turned into a beautiful green lawn with flower beds and shrubs all around it. The cottage itself had four sets of windows with little painted white shutters pinned back against the walls. Under each window was a window box full of geraniums and pansies. The roof had turned from grey to bright red and the stone walls were painted a soft cream colour. Smoke curled up from a tall red brick chimney.

'I want a house just like this when I grow up, Wonky,' said Molly, 'It's perfect.'

'Thank you for noticing,' said a gravelly voice.

Molly turned around to find the Fire Witch standing on the front doorstep with a frown on her face. She was dressed in a black witch's cloak and hat, her eyes were a very pale grey and her mouth was bright red. Molly thought she might be wearing lipstick.

'I like it,' said Molly. 'It's very pretty.'

The Fire Witch narrowed her eyes and stared at Molly. 'I don't think we've met, although you do look quite familiar. What is your name?'

'I'm Molly Miggins,' said Molly. She thought it best not to mention where she has seen the Fire Witch before.

'You had better come in I suppose, seeing as you've flown all this way… uninvited.'

Molly kept Wonky in her hand and stepped into the Fire Witch's front room. There was a flowery carpet on the floor, lace curtains in the windows and fancy, silk cushions on the sofa.

The Fire Witch noticed Molly's look of surprise. 'Did you think I lived in a cave or something?'

'I don't know what I thought,' said Molly. 'But I didn't expect it to look like Aunt Matilda's front room.'

'I like nice things,' said the Fire Witch. 'I bought all this stuff with me when I moved out here. You can't buy nice soft furnishings in the mountains.'

Molly agreed that it would be difficult.

The Fire Witch led Molly into the parlour which had a nice wooden table and four chairs tucked neatly under it. A nice sized window looked out over a beautifully kept garden which had a fountain, a rose bed and a large, glass greenhouse.

'How do you manage to grow all these plants out here?' asked Molly. 'I haven't seen them anywhere else in Splinge, not even at the palace.'

'Magic of course,' said the Fire Witch. 'You can grow anything if you use the right spells.' She cocked her head to one side and studied Molly's face. 'Do I know you from somewhere?' she asked.

'I don't think so,' said Molly. 'I haven't seen you before today.'

'It's that face… I'm sure I've seen it before…' The Fire Witch moved in for a closer look.

Molly didn't like being stared at. She took a step back

'I know,' screamed the witch. 'Hazel Whitewand. Do you know Hazel Whitewand?'

'She's my grandma,' said Molly quietly.

'HA,' cried the Fire Witch, 'I knew it. You look just like her.'

'I do not,' said Molly indignantly. 'She's got a wrinkly face and wobbly teeth and she slurps tea and…'

'The spitting image of her,' continued the witch. 'We were at school together.'

Molly smiled, 'That's nice.' She began to think things might take a turn for the better but she was to be disappointed.

'Hazel Whitewand… Do you know, she once sent me a *frog-eyes* spell wrapped up as a Christmas present? It meant I missed the Christmas party; I couldn't go looking like that. I had to wear swimming goggles to cover them up when I went to school; everyone thought it was hilarious.'

Molly gulped.

'The following year she got me with the *chicken leg* spell at the Academy sports day. I was in the hundred yards race and I was certain to win it. Half way down the track I developed chickens legs and I came in last.'

Molly held back a laugh.

'It's not funny,' said the Fire Witch. 'It wasn't funny then and it isn't funny now.'

'No,' agreed Molly, as she bit her cheek. 'It isn't.'

The Fire Witch watched Molly closely in case she as much as smirked. Molly did the nine times table in her head to try to keep the thought of the Fire Witch running down a race track with a pair of chicken legs. Eventually the Fire Witch changed the subject.

'Would you like a glass of lemonade?'

Molly nodded enthusiastically and when the Fire Witch went through to the kitchen to get it, she fired up Wonky.

'There's something not right about this, Wonky,' she said. 'The Fire Witch is being far too nice, and this place…' she opened her arms and turned a full circle, 'is too much like my Aunt Matilda's house to be real.'

'That's because it isn't real, Molly Miggins,' said the wand. 'She is taking thoughts from the back of your mind to make the rooms look comfortable and unthreatening. Try using the *cease illusion* spell again.'

Molly called, *cease illusion,* and the table and chairs, curtains and window disappeared leaving bare, grey stone walls and black flagstones behind them. In the corner, a steel, spiral staircase gave access to the upper floor. Molly walked into the kitchen but there was no sign of the Fire Witch. In the middle of the room was a large, bubbling, steaming, black cauldron that straddled a roaring fire. There was an ancient store cupboard with one of its doors hanging off, leaning unsteadily against the wall and a large stone sink with an old fashioned pump handle, built into the floor at the side of it. Molly stood by the sink and wondered how the Fire Witch had managed to get out of the room. As she turned around to look back at the kitchen, she heard a *plop* sound, and a witch's hat landed at her feet. Molly threw herself against the wall and looked up to see the Fire Witch hovering just below the ceiling. Her eyes were like hot coals, flames lapped around her mouth, she grinned a cruel grin and licked her lips.

'So, you have seen through my little illusion,' she croaked. Sholeh licked her lips again, fire danced around the edge of her tongue. 'I was hoping to have a little more fun with you than I have been allowed, but it doesn't really matter now.'

Molly addressed Wonky and backed towards the sink. 'Where is princess Ameera?' she asked.

'That's for me to know and you to find out,' snorted the Fire Witch. Smoke poured out of her nose, her eyes burned bright, she grinned again showing black, smoke-stained teeth and began to float slowly towards Molly.

Molly swung her wand into the air and fired a fire bolt. The spell hit Sholeh on the chest. The Fire Witch smiled, closed her eyes and soaked up the energy. 'Aaaah,' she said, 'a top up.'

'Bother,' said Molly as she realised her mistake. The Fire Witch shot a *flame thrower* spell; Molly threw herself to the floor, rolled over and got to her feet again all in one movement. She fired off a *freeze* spell but the Fire Witch had moved to the other end of the room and the spell hit the roof instead. Molly backed into the parlour and ran for the staircase as a sheet of flame roared through the doorway. She raced up the stairs firing *ice bolts* as she ran but the Fire Witch was wearing a protective, *heat* spell and the ice bolts sizzled and turned to vapour as they crashed into it.

When Molly reached the top of the stairs she found herself in a long room which had a number of steel chains fixed to thick iron rings on the wall. In the centre of the room was a steel-barred cage with a large padlock on the door. Inside was a girl of about ten years old. She stood up and came to the bars as Molly ran into the room.

'Who… What?' She stammered.

'I'm Molly Miggins,' panted Molly. 'I've come to…'

Her words were cut off as a searing ball of flame shot past her head. Molly ran behind the cage and dodged left and right to try to make the witch guess which way she would go.

The Fire Witch edged forward firing small pellets of fire. Molly managed to dodge most of them but the ones that did get through felt like the sting of an angry wasp.

'Ow,' she yelled. 'Ow.'

Molly made her own body armour with a *protect* spell, leapt out from behind the cage and fired an *ice slide* spell in front of Sholeh's feet. The Fire Witch stepped onto it and skated across the room with her arms flailing in the air. Molly fired an *ice bolt* spell at her toes and Sholeh's feet were knocked from underneath her. Steam rose from the ice slide as she tobogganed along, desperately trying to dig her fingernails into the ice to get some sort of grip. She screamed as she saw the steel cage loom up in front of her, a couple of seconds later she crashed into the metal cell, head first.

'Stand back,' Molly shouted. Ameera, moved away from the bars.

'Hurry, Molly Miggins,' she cried, 'the Fire Witch is getting up.'

Molly fired a *thunderbolt* spell at the padlock and blew it to pieces. She yanked the door open and grabbed the princess by the hand. 'Run,' she cried.

The Fire Witch got unsteadily to her knees as the girls ran for the stairs. She shook her head to clear it, then took aim and fired a *lightning bolt* spell. It crashed into the banister rail of the stairs and set it alight.

The princess skidded to a halt in front of the smoking stairway; Molly grabbed her arm and dragged her through the flames. 'Run and don't stop running until I catch up with you,' she told the princess.

On Wonky's advice, Molly fired an *ice sheet* spell. The three-inch thick ice sheet crackled as it crept across the floor towards the steel cage. The Fire Witch backed away and climbed onto the wooden bed as the ice spread into the cell, engulfing the bed legs.

'I'll find you, Molly Miggins,' she screamed as Molly disappeared down the stairs. 'You won't get far.'

The Fire Witch cast a *sunburst* spell that melted the ice on impact, sending a spray of steam into the air. Molly scampered through the house and found Ameera waiting by the front door. Molly threw it open and led the princess across the sharp black rocks at the front of the house. She picked up her broom and urged Ameera to climb on behind her.

'That spell won't hold her for long,' she warned.

Ameera straddled the broom and wrapped her arms around Molly's waist.

'Hold on tight, and whatever you do, don't let go,' said Molly. She hit the broom as hard as she could with her wand. '*FLY*,' she cried. '*Fly, Fly, Fly*.'

'The broom took off but flew erratically, Molly wasn't used to steering with the extra weight of another person on the broom, but she soon got the hang of it. She aimed the broom in the general direction of Castle Grey and settled to a steady speed. Suddenly she felt a blast of hot air on her cheek as a *fire bolt* spell whistled past her ear. Molly looked back to see the Fire Witch about two hundred yards behind and gaining fast. Molly knew they would never get to the castle before the Fire Witch caught them. Her brain went into overdrive, she needed a plan, and quickly.

Chapter Nineteen

Molly decided to turn around and try to fly back to the mountains. *At least we might find a cave or somewhere to hide from the Fire Witch back there,* she thought. She looked over her shoulder again, the Fire Witch had closed to fifty yards, another *fire bolt* whizzed over her hat.

'Hang on tight, I'm going to try something,' called Molly to the princess. 'Don't let go whatever you do.'

Molly tried to make it look like the broom was struggling by giving it little whacks with the wand to boost the speed for a few moments before allowing it to slow right down. She heard the Fire Witch cackle to herself as she slowed down herself, thinking she had caught them. When she was within touching distance of the back of her broom, Molly pushed the front of the handle down as far as it would go. The broom dropped and turned back on itself. For a few moments the girls flew upside down as they shot beneath the Fire Witch's broom. Molly straightened up and hit the broom three times with her wand.

'Fly, Fly, Fly,' she screamed. The broom jerked, then put on speed. When Molly looked back they were three hundred yards in front of the Fire Witch who was just coming out of a slow turn.

Molly headed for the mountains and again tried to bring the map she had seen on the wall in Castle Grey to mind. She closed her eyes and concentrated hard. When she opened them again the Fire Witch had closed to a two hundred yards and the *fire bolts* were flying again.

Molly saw the Fire Witch's house coming up ahead and steered the broom to the right. Half a mile further on she saw what she was looking for; the shadowy shape of a cave at the bottom of a deep ravine.

Molly allowed the broom to drop while she scanned the floor for a safe place to land. Her eyes came to rest on a narrow strip of land between two huge rock falls.

'This is going to be tight,' she called over her shoulder. 'I'd close my eyes if I were you.'

As the broom got closer to the ground they began to be buffeted by a wind that picked up strength as it was forced through the gap between the rocks. Molly slipped Wonky into her secret pocket and grabbed the broom handle with both hands. The wind did its best to force her onto the rocks on the right hand side of the gully, but Molly pushed left with all her strength and managed to pass through the gap with a foot to spare on either side.

She brought the broom in to land and they skidded across the rock strewn floor. Molly looked up as she climbed off the broom, half expecting to see the Fire Witch hovering above their heads, but she was nowhere to be seen.

Molly picked up her broom and led Ameera through the gulley to the cave she had spotted from the air. The girls had to climb over a huge pile of fallen rocks before they reached the entrance. Molly peered inside hoping she hadn't found the home of a dangerous, wild animal. She looked back to the sky but it appeared that the Fire Witch had been put off by the strong winds on the approach to the gorge. Molly pulled Wonky from her pocket and fired up the *glow in the dark* spell; she held the wand high in the air, took the princess's hand and walked slowly into the cave.

To Molly's relief there were no dead animal bones on the floor and it didn't look like it had ever been occupied. As they moved further into the cave she could hear the steady drip of water. She dropped to her hands and knees and crawled down a low tunnel which led into a huge, airy, cavern. Molly used a *bright light* spell and the cavern lit up as though it was in daylight. In front of her was a glistening rock pool fed by a steady stream of water that ran down the cavern wall. Molly scooped some water into her cupped hands and took a sip.

'That's lovely,' she exclaimed. 'The nicest water I've ever tasted.'

Ameera knelt down and scooped some into her mouth. 'Delicious,' she agreed.

Molly emptied her flask onto the floor and re-filled it with ice cool water from the pool, then she sat down with her back against the rock and pulled out the fruit that she had been given at the palace. She half-peeled a banana and handed it to Ameera.

'Why did you come for me, Molly Miggins?' asked the princess. 'You are not from our land.'

'It's a long and complicated story,' said Molly. 'I'll tell you all about it on the way home.' She yawned, took off her hat and lay down with her head on it. 'At the moment I just need to sleep.'

Ameera curled up with her head on Molly's legs. Molly curled her right hand around her wand and closed her eyes. 'Good night, Ameera,' she said. 'See you in the morning.'

*****

Molly awoke to the sound of screaming. She leapt to her feet, cast the *bright light* spell and looked for the source of the screams.

'So, you thought you could escape me with a bit of fancy flying, Molly Miggins.' The Fire Witch stood by the rock pool with Ameera at her feet. 'Well I know a trick or two as well, and I know every inch of these mountains.'

'What is it you want?' asked Molly. 'Your plans are in tatters now.'

'That's as maybe,' said Sholeh, 'but I still think I'll keep young Ameera. She may prove to be an asset yet. I'm sure her father will pay handsomely for her safe return. He may even be persuaded to give me a little bit of land near the palace… or even the palace itself.'

Sholeh patted Ameera on the head and cackled to herself.

'As for you, Molly Miggins, well, to be honest I haven't quite decided yet. I could use an apprentice if you fancy the job… No? Of course you don't. Everything is black or white, good or evil to you, but believe me there is far more to it than that. There are good witches, bad witches and some in between witches. You don't always have to be on one side or the other.'

'I know which side I'm on,' said Molly, 'and it's not yours.'

The Fire Witch cackled again. 'To tell you the truth, Molly Miggins, I don't really care one way or the other. You were lucky to get away with your little trick on Morgana, but you won't get away with it next time, take my word for it. She'll be back sooner rather than later and I intend to be in a good bargaining position when she does.'

Ameera kicked her legs and tried to get away from Sholeh. Molly thought about firing an *ice* spell but decided against it. The Fire Witch had her wand pointed directly at the head of the princess and she didn't want to risk her being hurt.

Suddenly, she heard Wonky's voice in her head. 'Molly Miggins, can you hear me? Don't speak if you can, just think your reply.'

Yes, I can hear you clearly, Wonky, I don't understand how though.

'As I told you before, I helped to write the Big Book of Spells. One of those spells enables me to use thought transference. It's called the *telepathy* spell. I'm using it now. Handy isn't it?'

It's brilliant, Wonky. But is there a spell in the Big Book of Spells that will get us out of this mess?

'I'm sure there is, Molly Miggins, we just need to bide our time.'

The Fire Witch took Molly's silence to be a sign of submission. 'Lost your tongue, eh?' she cackled. 'Well you could lose more than that soon because I'm just thinking about whether to keep you locked in a fire cage, so I can come and laugh at you every morning, or just frazzle you with a fire bomb right now. Ooh, it's just too hard, I can't decide.'

Molly lowered her wand slightly and waited for advice from Wonky. The Fire Witch noticed the movement and pointed her wand at Ameera again.

'Don't do anything stupid or I'll warm the princess up a bit with a *microwave* spell.'

Sholeh pointed the wand to her feet and drew a line of flames on the floor. 'Don't try the *ice* spell again either; I'm ready for it this time.' The Fire Witch began to glow; her eyes turned a deep red and flames licked about her head and shoulders. She grabbed Ameera by the collar and dragged her to her feet.

'I'll just put this little pest to sleep for a few minutes and then you can have my full attention. It's a shame that you'll never make more than a junior witch; you did show quite a lot of promise. I'll give your love to Morgana the next time we meet; she'll be so jealous that I got to you before she could.'

'I've got the spell ready, Molly Miggins,' Wonky's voice was steady and confident. 'One of the spells in the Big Book of Spells is the *water spout* spell. It can be used in lots of ways but in our circumstances I think it would best to aim the spell directly at the rock pool. You won't need to be too accurate with this one.'

The Fire Witch held Ameera with one hand and lifted her wand to cast the *sleep* spell but before she could utter a word, Molly pointed Wonky at the rock pool and shouted, *water spout.*

The pool began to bubble, then rumble. A huge spout of water, ten feet wide, shot straight up into the air. It hit the roof of the cavern and poured gallons of water down onto the Fire Witch's head. Sholeh screamed as the deluge poured over her. Her head sizzled and great clouds of steam erupted from her body. She took a step backwards and waved her arms around in a vain attempt to fight off the torrent of water. Her wand fell to the floor; she covered her eyes, took another step back and fell into the erupting pool.

As Sholeh thrashed about in the water, Molly pointed her wand at the raging pool and called, *cease spout.*

She ran to Ameera to see if she was hurt, but apart from a bruise or two the princess was fine. Molly picked up The Fire Witch's wand, slipped it into her secret pocket and walked to the edge of the pool.

Sholeh's head broke the surface of the water; she gasped for air and flailed her arms. 'I can't swim,' she gurgled. 'Help me.'

'I don't see why I should,' said Molly. 'You were going to frazzle me a moment ago.'

'I won't frazzle you, I promise,' said Sholeh. 'Please get me out of here. My fire's gone out.'

Molly and Ameera offered a hand each and pulled the shaking, shivering Sholeh from the pool. She lay on the stone floor in a soggy mess, gasping for air. When she had recovered somewhat, Molly pulled the Fire Witch's wand from her secret pocket and threw it into the pool.

‘Why did you do that,’ wailed Sholeh. ‘I’ll never find it in there.’
‘I know,’ said Molly. ‘You won’t be able to cause any more trouble without it.’

Molly helped Sholeh to her feet and led the princess and the former Fire Witch out of the cavern. As she stood in the cave entrance, she saw a dozen Grey Academy witches flying towards them.

Molly waved. ‘We’re here, Aspen,’ she called.

Ten minutes later Molly was surrounded by Grey Academy witches. Her back had never received so many pats in her whole life.

‘Sylvia thought you might need a bit of assistance, Molly,’ said a witch called Cecile, ‘but it appears that she was wrong.’

Molly found her broom and straddled it. Cecile offered to carry Ameera, but the princess declined. ‘I’d like to fly with Molly again if that’s all right?’

Molly smiled and shuffled forward. Ameera climbed on and hugged Molly's waist.

'What about me, you can't just leave me here. I'll starve to death without my wand,' cried Sholeh.

After a hasty discussion Molly suggested that Sholeh should be allowed to ride with Cecile and the witches set off for The Grey Academy.

Chapter Twenty

At Castle Grey, Sholeh was put into the dungeon with Livia and the ten or so witches that had been stripped of their power. Molly had a hot bath and went for lunch with the rest of the Academy witches. She was cheered into the room and cheered out of it again, much to her embarrassment.

Sylvia was waiting for her in the entrance hall when she came out from lunch. The entire Academy formed two lines and raised their wands to form a guard of honour that Molly had to walk through to reach the High Witch.

'Molly Miggins, esteemed witch of the White Academy, the students of the Castle Grey wish to offer you their grateful thanks for all that you have done, not only for us, but for the land of Splinge and beyond.'

The witches applauded loudly. Molly blushed again.

Sylvia handed Molly the Big Book of Spells and a report scroll that detailed the events at the Academy, before, during and after Molly's arrival.

'The Magic Council have to know what happened here,' she said. 'I have asked for a replacement for Livia and I've proposed that we begin a major student and tutor exchange program with the White Academy so that this sort of thing can never happen again.'

A witch stepped forward holding a red satin cushion. Silvia picked up a gold medallion, engraved with the crest of the Grey Academy and hung it around Molly's neck.

'It gives me great pleasure to award an honorary membership of the Grey Academy of Witches to Molly Miggins. The Academy wishes you every success in your future studies and we will welcome you back with open arms should you pass this way again. Your name will be added to the Academy roll of honour.'

Sylvia bowed, the witches applauded and Molly blushed all over again.

It was decided that ten witches would accompany Molly back to the royal palace. Aspen, who had been given two weeks holiday, was one of them. She was charged with carrying the Big Book of Spells.

Molly said her final goodbyes to Sylvia at the main gates of the Academy. 'What will you do with Livia, Sholeh and the other witches?' she asked.

'We don't really know what to do with them,' said Sylvia. 'I suppose they'll have to stay where they are.'

'Let them go,' suggested Molly. 'They're not a threat any more. They have no wands and no power. Give them some food and water and send them on their way.'

'If that is what you advise then that's what we will do,' said Sylvia. She clapped her hands and issued orders.

Molly turned away from the castle that had been the scene of such a big part of her adventure and looked around to see if her companions were ready, then she pulled Wonky from her pocket and hit the broom hard.

'*FLY!*' she cried.

Molly and her entourage were spotted long before they reached the outskirts of the town and by the time they came in to land there was a large crowd of people waiting to greet them. Molly was treated to a huge round of applause as she landed with the princess on the courtyard outside the palace gates.

Aspen spotted her mother and father standing with Erin at the front of the crowd and ran to greet them. Other witches with families in the town spotted smiling faces and hurried across the courtyard to be welcomed with hugs and tears.

Molly stood hand in hand with Ameera while the townspeople threw flower petals over them. A few moments later the palace gates opened and the king walked into the courtyard followed by a group of his advisors.

Ameera ran to the king and threw herself into his arms. Tears poured down the king's face. Molly looked at the floor and thought about home.

After a while, the king wiped his eyes and held up his hand for silence.

'Molly Miggins,' he said. 'My family will be forever grateful to you, not just for rescuing my beloved daughter, but for showing us what can be achieved if a person is determined and brave.'

The king clapped his hands and a young girl of Molly's age, stepped forward carrying a silver plate that held a large gold brooch. The king picked up the brooch and pinned it onto Molly's tunic. 'Molly Miggins, I bestow upon you the title, Hero of Splinge.'

'Molly Miggins, Molly Miggins,' chanted the crowd.

When the crowd had calmed down, the king took Molly to one side and asked if there was anything he could give her as a personal reward, but Molly couldn't think of anything she really needed.

'Is Ratruhn still in the tower?' she asked. 'He didn't do that much wrong really; he was only protecting you and the people of the town, even if he did get a bit above himself.'

'Yes, he's still in the tower, would you have me release him?'

'I think so,' said Molly. 'You could give him his old job back if he promises not to do anything like that again.'

'It shall be done, Molly Miggins,' said the king. He nodded to one of his advisors who walked down to the guardhouse.

The king handed Molly a scroll and an ornate wooden box with a gold lock.

'Here is a gift for your Magic Council; it contains small jars of very rare spices that cannot easily be found in your land. They can be used to make powerful magic spells. Please tell your wizard that we send them with our thanks.'

Molly put the scroll in her secret pocket with the one that Sylvia had given her. She wondered how she was supposed to carry the box, the Big Book of Spells and fly at the same time. She asked the king if one of the witches could escort her to the portal.

'You can have as many escorts as you wish to have, Molly Miggins,' said the king. He leaned over and whispered in Molly's ear. 'There is one last favour you can do me if you wouldn't mind?'

'Anything,' said Molly. 'Just name it.'

'When you arrived in our land, you were given the task of delivering a parcel and escorting a young girl back through the portal with you, were you not?'

'I was,' said Molly. 'I've failed in that part of the task though. I'm going back alone.'

'Not necessarily,' said the king. 'I have received a request from one of my subjects who wishes to attend the White Academy. She was due to study at Castle Grey with her sister but she has asked special permission to be allowed to leave with you. I have given my consent providing that you agree.'

Erin stepped out of the crowd. 'It's me, Molly, if you don't mind.'

A huge grin spread across Molly's face. 'I'd be delighted to take you, Erin. I'm sure the White Academy will accept your application.

I'd love to see you at school every day too, we can laugh at Henrietta, she thinks she's the top dog but she's hopeless really.'

Erin gave Molly a big hug and turned to her family.

'Molly Miggins said yes!' Erin ran back to her mother and sister to say her goodbyes.

The crowd cheered again and again as Molly, escorted by Aspen, Erin and Cecile, took off from the palace courtyard. Out to sea, Molly could see a rowing boat with two people in it pull away from the tower.

They arrived at the gateway to the Halfway House without incident. Erin climbed off her sister's broom and walked with Molly to the stone wall at the side of the Gateway. Molly waved goodbye to Cecile and Aspen and handed her broom to Erin.

'You'll need one of these in a year or so and this is a particularly good one,' she said.

Erin took the broom from Molly with a big smile. 'I'll look after it,' she said.

Molly took Wonky from her secret pocket and moved it from right to left over the White Academy crest. A thick mist descended and a black space appeared in the wall. Molly placed the king's gift box on top of the Big Book of Spells and held them in front of her. Erin slipped her arm though Molly's and together they walked into the portal.

The girls came out of the other side of the portal into thick, grey cloud and drizzly rain.

'Welcome to my land,' said Molly. 'You'll see a lot of this wet stuff.'

As the portal closed behind them Molly heard a voice she recognised instantly. ‘Molly Miggins, you have returned, is the task complete?’

‘Sort of,’ said Molly. She grinned at Erin and handed the gift box, the Big Book of Spells and the report scrolls to the wizard. ‘It’s a long and complicated story.’

The End

7537851R00071

Printed in Germany
by Amazon Distribution
GmbH, Leipzig